MADAGASCAR™

MOVIE NOVEL

MADAGASCAR™

MOVIE NOVEL

By Louise Gikow

SCHOLASTIC INC.

New York   Toronto   London
Auckland   Sydney   Mexico City
New Delhi   Hong Kong   Buenos Aires

DREAMWORKS
ANIMATION SKG

ISBN: 0-439-69623-2

Madagascar TM & © 2005 DreamWorks Animation L.L.C.

Published by Scholastic Inc.
SCHOLASTIC and associated logos are trademarks and/or registered trademarks of Scholastic Inc.

12 11 10 9 8 7 6 5 4 3 2   5 6 7 8 9 10/0

Designed by Joseph R. Williams
Printed in the U.S.A.
First printing, May 2005

CHAPTER ONE

The sun began to rise.

The sky was shot with threads of gold and red as the great yellow orb flooded the bright green foliage with morning light.

Suddenly, a magnificent zebra flew across the landscape on a long, green vine like a black-and-white striped Tarzan. He landed in a clearing surrounded by exotic tropical plants. He hit the ground running and headed for the edge of a chasm, where dozens of penguins flying in formation awaited them.

At the edge of the chasm, the zebra didn't hesitate. Gathering his four legs beneath him, he jumped powerfully over it, sailing high in the air. He did a graceful forward roll and then another as his front hooves scrambled to grab the other side of the cliff.

He came up short.

Tumbling over and over, he fell into the chasm.

Then, just in time, four penguins appeared and positioned themselves just under his hooves. Pumping their little wings, they flew him up and over to the other side.

The zebra, with a nod of thanks to the penguins, continued on his journey across the jungle landscape.

Behind him, a powerful lion arose from some bushes, his eyes glinting. He raced silently after the zebra.

The zebra didn't notice the lion. He continued to run. As he approached a lake in which the glowing orange sun was reflected, he shook his handsome head and glanced around him.

The lion's powerful strides brought him closer . . . closer . . .

It was a beautiful day, the zebra thought, and things could only get better. After all, he was the most graceful, the fleetest, the most intelligent animal in the jungle. There was nothing he couldn't do. No situation he couldn't handle. No predator who could take him by —

"Surprise!"

"Aaaaaaagh!"

The zebra — Marty by name — tumbled off the treadmill he was riding as Alex, a powerful-looking lion, reared up in front of him.

"Alex!" Marty picked himself up and shook his head. "You almost gave me a heart attack." He pointed to a mural across from his cage, located in New York City's Zoo. The mural showed the jungles of Africa. Then he gestured to the treadmill.

"Not while I'm on the treadmill," he said, checking his legs to make sure he was all right. "When the zebra's in the zone, leave him alone. I was just racing through the jungles of my homeland, fleet as a gazelle —"

"Gee, Marty, I'm sorry," Alex said, not looking sorry at all. "I didn't mean to mess up your workout. I just wanted to be the first to wish you a happy birthday."

Marty's mouth hung open. Then he smiled. "Hey, thanks, man," he said.

"And . . ." Alex opened his mouth to reveal rows of razor-sharp teeth. "I've got something stuck in between my molar and my bicuspid. It's driving me crazy. Can you help me out here? Please?"

Marty nodded, sticking his head in Alex's mouth. "You came to the right place, my friend," he said, his voice muffled. "Dr. Marty, D.D.S., is in the house."

Marty peered around inside Alex's mouth. "Uh, I don't see anything," he began.

"It's on the left," Alex said.

"Ow!" Marty pulled his head out of Alex's mouth. "Don't talk with your mouth full, okay?"

"Sorry," Alex said.

"Apology accepted. Open wide now . . ."

Alex opened wide, and Marty stuck his head back inside his mouth. "Ah-hah!" he said suddenly. "I see something . . . right here!"

Marty reached in . . . and pulled out a beautifully-wrapped present.

"What the heck was this doing in there?" he said, shaking it. "No wonder you were having problems —"

"Happy Birthday!" Alex yelled.

"Oh!" Marty blushed. "Thanks, man!"

Marty started to open the present — not an easy thing to do when you have hooves.

"Here — let me." Alex grabbed it from Marty and ripped the paper to shreds with his teeth. Inside was a beautiful snow globe of New York City, complete with a miniature Alex in the middle perched on a rock. It said "City Zoo" on its base.

"These aren't even in stores yet," Alex said proudly. "Here, check it out!" He shook the snow globe, and little white flakes rained down on the miniature Alex. "Look at that. Oooh, look at that!"

"Look at that." Marty nodded. "It's snowing."

"Ten years old!" Alex said, shaking the snow globe again and grinning at Marty. "You're ten years old. A decade. Double digits! The big one-oh!"

Marty nodded again. He didn't look very happy.

Alex frowned. "You don't like the globe?"

Marty shook his head. "No, no, it's great," he said.

Alex's shoulders slumped. "You hate it. I should have gotten you that Alex alarm clock. That's the big seller. . . ."

Marty took the snow globe from Alex and walked over to a pile of stuff — calendars, coffee cups, golf clubs, Frisbees — all boasting pictures of Alex on them, and all gifts from Alex.

He put the snow globe on top.

"No, no, the present's great," he said to Alex. "It's just that another year has come and gone, and I'm still just doing the same old thing. Stand over here, trot over there, eat some grass, walk back over here. . . ."

"I see your problem," Alex nodded.

Marty sighed. "Maybe I should go to law school —"

Alex shook his head. "You just need to break out of that boring routine."

Marty scratched his hoof on the ground. "How?" he asked.

Alex thought for a moment. "Throw out the old act," he said finally. "Get out there. Who knows what you're gonna do? Make it up as you go along. Ad-lib, improvise on the fly. Boom, boom, boom!"

Marty looked doubtful. "Really?" he said.

"Yeah," Alex answered. "Make it fresh!"

"Fresh, huh?" Marty said slowly. "Okay. I can do fresh."

"It works for me!" Alex said cheerfully.

Bong! Bong! Bong!

The clock at the entrance chimed.

Alex flexed his claws. "Here come the people, Marty," he said excitedly. "Oh, I love the people! It's fun people fun time! Whoa! See ya!"

Alex bounded out of Marty's enclosure and over the fence. He landed on the rear end of Gloria the hippo, who was submerged in the pool of water in the center of her enclosure.

"Let's go, Gloria. Up and at 'em!" Alex yelled. "We're open!"

Gloria's ears — the only other parts of her that weren't underwater — flicked once. Then she slowly raised her bulk up, revealing her massive head and body. She gave a giant yawn.

"What day is it?" she asked.

"It's Friday! Field trip day!" Alex caroled. "Let's go! Come on! All those little school kids are waiting for us to thrill 'em!"

"Field trip day. Let's get up and go. . . ." Gloria murmured, sinking back under the water. She snored mightily, and bubbles floated to the surface.

Alex shook his mane and shrugged. He leaped out of Gloria's enclosure and onto the roof of the giraffe house.

"Melman, Melman, Melman, Melman, Melman, Melman!" he crooned. "Wake up! Rise and shine! It's another fabulous morning in the Big Apple. Let's go!"

Melman the giraffe walked out of his house. He wore a tissue box on each of his hooves and an anti-scratch collar on his head. He looked miserable.

"Not for me," he said, sneezing. "I'm calling in sick."

"What?" Alex stopped short, shocked.

"I found . . . *another* brown spot on my shoulder. See? Right here. Right here, you see?"

Melman craned his long neck around to show Alex the spot.

Alex shook his head. "Melman. You have brown spots all *over* you. You're a *giraffe*!"

Bong! Bong! Bong! The zoo clock finished chiming the hour. The gates opened, and crowds of people began streaming into the zoo, dumping half-eaten bagels, half-empty cups of coffee, and newspapers into the trash.

Over in the chimp enclosure, Mason the chimp grabbed a bagel, a half a cup of coffee, and the sports section out of a nearby trash can. He slapped another chimp, Phil, with the paper and handed him the coffee.

"Phil, wake up, you filthy monkey!" Mason chattered.

Phil gave him a dirty look and took a sip of coffee. It had artificial sweetener in it. He spit it out.

Back in the zebra enclosure, Marty was getting ready for another day at the zoo. "Oh, I'm gonna be fresh," he said to himself, inspecting his hooves. "Straight out of the ground. Freshalicious." He took a drink of water, gargled, and spit it out. "Ziploc fresh!"

Behind the big artificial rock that stood in the center of his enclosure, Alex warmed up as an announcer spoke over the PA system. People were already three-deep in front of his lair. This was Alex's favorite part of the day — his entrance.

"Superstar! And I'm gonna go far!" he muttered to himself, pacing around, warming up his vocal muscles. "Red leather, yellow leather. Red leather, yellow leather. Red leather, yellow leather." He stretched, pushing his front paws out in front of him, and flicked his tail.

"Ladies and gentlemen, children of all ages." The announcer's voice crackled. "The City Zoo proudly presents the king of New York City —"

Alex mouthed the words along with the announcer. "Alex the lion!"

"It's show time!" Alex said happily. He crouched down low. Then he sprang up and landed on the rock. He struck a majestic pose.

An electric fan blew his mane back as fireworks erupted around him. The crowd cheered. Cameras clicked and whirred.

Alex grinned and posed. *Does it get any better than this*? he thought to himself.

Over in the zebra enclosure, people were still gathering. Marty took a deep breath and plastered on a big smile.

"Gather round, people!" he said. "Big zebra show about to start!"

He strutted back and forth, moonwalking and tossing his head. The crowd ooohed and aaahed.

"Check out the zebra, takin' care of business!" Marty trumpeted.

He dunked his head into his water trough and came up with a mouthful of H_2O. Lifting his head, he sprayed the crowd. Little kids giggled and screamed as adults grabbed for their handkerchiefs and dabbed at their suits.

Next door, Gloria swam and spun in her pool as people watched, open-mouthed.

In the giraffe house, three veterinarians hovered over Melman, who closed his eyes blissfully.

And in the penguin cage, the penguins were doing their usual "waddle 'n' wave," as Skipper called it. Skipper was their leader. He knew the zoo routine inside out, and hated every minute of it. He intended to break out and head for Antarctica just as soon as he could.

"Just smile and wave, boys, smile and wave," he muttered to his troops. "Remember — we're blowing this joint as soon as the tunnel is done!" Then he called down to Kowalski, his second lieutenant.

"Kowalski!" he barked. "Progress report!"

"We're only five hundred feet from the main sewer line, " Kowalski said.

"And the bad news?" Skipper squinted down at Kowalski.

Kowalski held up a plastic spoon. "We've broken our last shovel," he said.

"Right." Skipper looked around. "Rico?"

Another one of the penguins separated himself from the group and waddled over. He gave Skipper a crisp salute.

"Yes?" he said snappily.

"You're on litter patrol," Skipper told him. "We need shovels. And find more Popsicle sticks. We need them to shore up the tunnel. I don't want to risk another cave-in."

"Yes, sir!" Rico saluted and dived into the penguin pool.

"How 'bout me, Skipper?"

Skipper looked down at a cute and cuddly penguin.

"I want you to look cute and cuddly, Private," he said. "Today, we're gonna blow this dump."

Back at the zebra enclosure, Marty was doing armpit farts.

"Yeah!" he said as three five-year-olds put their hands under their arms and flapped like crazy. "You don't see that on Animal Planet!"

A few grown-ups groaned and dragged their kids away.

Marty called after them. "Show's over, folks. Thanks for coming. I hope you thought it was fresh. I'll be here all week. In fact, I'll be here for my whole life, 365 days a year, including Christmas, Chanukah, Halloween, and Kwanzaa." Marty raised his voice.

After the last of the people were out of sight, Marty settled down in the corner of his pen, grabbing his "Alex the Lion" collector cup. It was empty. He tossed it aside —

Suddenly, a white plastic spoon burst up from the ground. A hole opened up, and four penguin heads popped out.

"You! Quadruped!" Skipper yelled. "Sprechen zi English?"

Marty scratched his head.

"I sprechen," he said.

"What continent is this?" Skipper demanded.

"Manhattan," Marty said.

Skipper's face fell. "Hoover dam!" he yelled. "We're still in New York. Abort! Dive! Dive! Dive!"

All four penguins started to sink back into the hole. Marty ran over.

"Wait a minute!" he said. "Hey, you in the tux!"

The penguins stopped.

"What are you guys doing?" Marty asked.

"We're digging a tunnel to Antarctica," Private said excitedly.

"Ant-hootica?" Marty said, confused.

Skipper gestured for Marty to come closer. "Can you keep a secret, my monochromatic friend?" he asked.

Marty nodded.

"Have you ever seen any penguins running free around New York City?" Skipper went on. "Of course not. We don't belong here! It's just not natural! It's all some kind of whacked-out conspiracy."

Skipper lowered his voice, glancing around to make sure no one was nearby. "We're headed for the wide open spaces of Antarctica. To the wild!"

"The wild?" Marty's eyes opened wide. "You can actually *go* there? That sounds great! Where is this place? Tell me where it is —"

But the penguins had already vanished.

Marty sat down again, stunned. He looked up at the painting on his enclosure wall. The bright green grasses waved, beckoning to him like a beautiful melody playing faintly in the distance.

He had always thought that it was just a picture — that the wild wasn't actually real.

Had he been wrong?

CHAPTER TWO

Later that same day, it was time for Alex's last show of the day.

He stood in his enclosure, gathering himself for his big entrance as the crowd waited outside, waiting in breathless anticipation.

The tinny announcer's voice blared. "For his final appearance of the day . . . the king of New York City . . . Alex the Lion!"

Alex whipped around, opened his mouth, and let loose with a magnificent, earth-shaking roar.

The crowd went wild. Flashbulbs flashed. Fireworks exploded. Grown men wept. Children cheered. People of all ages showered Alex with roses.

The clock chimed five o'clock.

Alex bowed modestly. "Thank you! Thank you very much! You are a great crowd. Give yourselves a hand. Thank you! Everybody get home safe now!"

The crowd settled down. Then the people slowly filed out of the zoo.

Alex licked his lips. "Suppertime!" He grinned toothily.

He, Marty, Gloria, and Melman gathered in the neighboring corners of their enclosures as dinner was delivered.

A well-marbled cut of grade-A sirloin steak on a silver platter arrived at Alex's den. Zoo workers combed and dried his mane as he lay on the top of his wall, chewing on the bone.

"Mmm. Tasty," he muttered.

Marty lifted the silver dome on his plate to reveal a perfect square of Kentucky blue grass.

Gloria nibbled on an assortment of fruit while a zoo worker gave her a deep-tissue massage.

"This is the life," she sighed.

Melman, acupuncture needles sticking out of him every which way, downed his forty vitamin pills.

"Oh, I'm in heaven!" he sighed.

Some wrapped presents were stacked in the corner of Marty's enclosure. He started to open one.

"Oooh, it's Marty's birthday!" Gloria sang. "Whatcha got, whatcha got, whatcha got?"

Marty finished tearing off the wrapping paper and opened the box.

"Ahh, a thermometer. Thanks, I love it, Melman. I love it."

"Okay, okay, Gloria, get the cake," Alex said. "Melman, c'mon!"

Gloria disappeared behind her wall as Melman blew a party horn to get them in tune.

"Happy birthday to you! Happy birthday to you! You look like a monkey . . . and you smell like one, too!"

Over in the monkey cage, Phil frowned, sniffed his armpit, and passed out.

Gloria emerged with Marty's birthday cake. Multi-colored candies were stuck all over it. A big 10 candle burned on top.

Marty blushed. "Ah, well now. You guys are just embarrassing me and yourselves. . . ."

Alex shook his mane. "What are you talking about? We worked on that cake all last week!"

"Make a wish, babycakes," Gloria urged.

Marty thought for a moment. He closed his eyes and blew out the candles.

Then he took a big bite of the cake. Frosting and candy stuck to his muzzle.

"What'd ya wish for?" Alex asked.

Marty shook his head, chewing. "Nope! I can't tell you that."

Alex put on his most appealing face. "C'mon, tell," he urged.

"No sir-ee," Marty said, snorting. "It's bad luck!"

Melman bent his head down and licked delicately at the icing. "That's just a superstition," he said. He stopped short. "Although I do believe in superstitions," he added worriedly.

Alex glanced over at Melman. "You know, it's bad luck to believe in superstitions," he said innocently.

Melman blinked.

Marty scratched his hind leg. "You want some bad luck? I'll blab it out. If you wanna be safe, I'll keep my mouth shut."

Gloria snorted. "Oh, for crying out loud, Marty, would you just tell us? I mean really. What could happen?"

Marty nodded. "Okay," he said, taking a deep breath. "I wished I could go to the wild."

"The wild?" Alex started to laugh. He laughed so hard that he fell back off his wall.

Melman choked on the party horn.

"Told you it was bad luck," Marty said, shrugging.

Alex bounded back onto his wall.

"The wild? Are you nuts?" he said. "That is crazy!"

"It's unsanitary," Melman added.

Marty stretched out his neck stubbornly. "The penguins are going, so why can't I?" he asked.

"The penguins are psychotic," Alex said dryly.

"C'mon." Marty stood up and started to pace around. "It would be great! Imagine going back to nature, back to your roots. Clean air, wide open spaces. . . ."

"I hear they have wide open spaces in Connecticut," Gloria said.

"Connecticut?" Marty stopped short. "How do you get to Connecticut?"

Melman thought for a moment. "You'd have to go down to Grand Central, then take the Metro North train —"

Marty was intrigued. "So one could take the train —"

"Marty, c'mon." Alex shook his head. "What would Connecticut have to offer us?"

"Lyme disease," Melman said gloomily.

"Thank you, Melman," Alex said. "For once, you have a point."

Marty frowned and pawed at the dirt. "No, no, really. I just —"

Alex held up the remains of his steak. There wasn't much left.

"There's certainly none of this in the wild," he said. "This is a highly refined . . . type of food . . . thing. That you do not find in the wild."

He gnawed gently on a piece of gristle before dropping the steak on his plate.

Marty stared at Alex. "You never thought there might be more to life than steak, Alex?" he asked.

Alex looked down at the steak. "He didn't mean that, baby," he said. "No, no, no." He picked up the steak and held it out to Marty. "Marty, say you're sorry to my steak."

Marty ignored him. "Doesn't it ever bother you that you don't know anything about life outside this zoo?"

Alex, Gloria, and Melman looked at one another.

They all shook their heads.

Alex stared at Marty.

"Uh, Marty?"

Marty looked at Alex hopefully. If only Alex thought going to the wild was a good idea —

"You got a little schmutz on your nose," Alex said, squinting at Marty.

Marty sighed and licked the frosting off his face.

"Thanks, guys," he said sadly. "Thanks for the party. It was great. Really."

Marty turned and went over to his treadmill. He got on and started trotting.

The other three animals stared after him.

"What's eating him?" Melman asked.

Gloria shook her head. "Maybe you should speak to him, Alex," she suggested. "You know. Go over there and give him a little pep talk."

"Hey." Alex tossed the steak bone behind him. "I already gave him a snow globe."

Gloria rolled her eyes. "Alex . . ."

Melman yawned. "Well, I can see where this is going," he said. "It's getting late. I guess I'm gonna go to sleeeeeep . . ."

Melman snored, his head dropping to one side of his long neck.

Gloria turned, giving Alex a look as she walked back towards her pool. "Talk to him!" she mouthed.

Then she turned to Marty.

"Night, Marty," she called. "Happy Birthday!"

"Night, Glo," Marty replied, glancing over his shoulder as he picked up the pace a bit on the treadmill. "Thanks again."

Gloria slid into the water with a splash. Alex got his umbrella up just in time.

She gave Alex a look, gesturing to Marty again. Alex made a face. Then she submerged.

Alex sighed. If he didn't talk to Marty, he'd never hear the end of it.

He looked over at his friend, who was wistfully gazing at the picture on his wall as he clocked off the miles.

"What a day," Alex said conversationally. "The food, the fans, the pampering. Pampering, food, fans. I mean, really. I tell you — it just doesn't get any better than this."

He stretched and glanced up. "Oooh, it just did! Even the star is out."

Marty looked up. A single star twinkled in the New York sky.

"You're not going to find a star like that in the wild," Alex pointed out.

Marty grunted. "It's a helicopter," he said.

Alex looked up at the star. It flew off.

He looked back over at Marty.

"Marty, buddy," he said. "Listen. Everyone has days when they think the grass might be greener somewhere else, but I happen to know, on great authority, that grass sucks. I'll take cement any day of the week. Grass comes and goes. Cement isn't going anywhere. You can trust cement."

Marty stopped running, got off the treadmill and turned to face Alex.

"Come on," he said. "How do you really, absolutely know that there isn't some place better than here? At least admit there's a possibility. . . ."

Alex shook his head.

Marty walked over to Alex's wall. "Just give me a maybe," he went on. "A 'could be.' A snowball's chance. A one in a million. A needle in a haystack . . ."

Marty reached over and grabbed Alex's head, forcing him to nod up and down.

"Uh-huh. Yeah. Okay, already," Alex said.

Marty grinned. But as soon as he let go, Alex shook his head again.

Marty looked around at his enclosure. It was nice . . . but it was still a cage, no matter how you looked at it.

"Just look at me," he said to Alex. "I'm ten years old, Alex. My life is half over, and I don't even know if I'm black with white stripes or white with black stripes. There's gotta be more to being a zebra than this.

Alex looked at him. "Marty," he said slowly. "Do you think some other place is going to tell you who you are? I'll tell you who you are. You're my best friend. Are you going to leave me and all your friends behind?"

Alex gazed at Marty appealingly.

Marty thought for a minute. Then he nodded excitedly.

"Hey. You're right," he said. "Let's go together!"

Alex frowned. "What?" he asked. "Go where?"

"The wild!" Marty said, excited. "C'mon. You and me! Together! It's a straight shot down Fifth Avenue to Grand Central. We'll grab a train and head north . . . we can be back by morning. No one will ever know!"

Alex stared at his best friend. "You're joking, right?"

Marty stopped short. His heart sank. His shoulders slumped.

"Yeah, I'm joking," he said finally. "Of course I'm joking. Give me a break. Like we're ever gonna get on a train. . . ."

Alex sighed with relief. "Don't do that!" he said. "You really had me worried there . . ."

Marty nodded. "Ah, well, I guess I'll hit the sack."

Alex nodded. "Me, too. I'll need to rest my voice for tomorrow. It's Senior's Day, you know. I have to roar extra loud. Give 'em a little jolt. You know what I'm talking about?"

Alex hopped down off the wall into his enclosure.

"Night, Ali-al." Marty turned and wandered back towards his treadmill.

Alex clapped his hands and a space heater turned on. He settled down and shut his eyes.

The noise of the jungle twittered and screeched around him.

"Aw, they forgot to turn off the ambient sound again," Alex groaned.

"Don't worry. I got it." Marty kicked at the wall and the jungle noises disappeared, replaced by the sirens and car alarms that were the city's soundtrack.

Alex sighed. "Ah, much better."

He started to snore.

Marty stood there, staring at his mural. He hadn't been kidding about leaving the zoo, of course. If Alex had said yes, he would have been on the eleven forty-five to Greenwich at the drop of a —

Oh, what difference did it make? He was never going to see the wild. He might as well get used to the fact that he was stuck here in New York City for the rest of his life.

Marty stared at his mural.

Or was he . . . ?

CHAPTER THREE

"Alex! Alex!"

Alex rolled over in his sleep. He was dreaming of a steak. A nice, juicy filet mignon with just a little fat around the edges. He drooled, sucking his thumb.

"Alex!!!"

Alex rolled over onto his side. "Wha?" he groaned, opening one eye.

Melman's nose was two inches away from his. The giraffe looked extremely upset.

"Okay," he blabbered. "You know how I always wake up every two hours? Well, I got up, and I happened to look over at Marty's pen, which I usually don't do, I don't know why, but I did, and this time I looked over and —"

Alex opened the other eye. "What, Melman? What's going on?"

"It's Marty!" Melman hissed. "He's gone!"

Alex's eyes opened wide. "Gone? What do you mean, *gone?*"

A minute later, Alex, Melman, and Gloria were staring at the penguin hole in Marty's pen in total disbelief.

"How long has he been working on this?" Melman said. He stuck his head into the hole. "Marty? Marty!"

Gloria flapped her ears. "That hole is too small," she said, shaking her head. "He wouldn't fit down there."

Behind them, Alex was tearing apart the straw that made up Marty's bed.

"Marty? Marty? Where are you, buddy?"

Gloria shook her heavy head. "This doesn't make any sense," she said. "Where would he go?"

Alex turned. "Connecticut!" he said grimly.

Gloria's eyes widened. "He wouldn't!" she gasped.

"He would," Alex snapped.

"Oh no!" Melman said, tying his neck into a knot. "What are we going to do? We gotta call somebody!"

Alex raced over to a pay phone near Marty's pen.

He picked it up and began to dial.

Then he hung it up again.

"Wait a second," he said slowly. "We can't call the people. They'll be really mad. It'll get Marty transferred. You don't bite the hand that feeds you!"

Gloria nodded. "I know *that's* right," she said.

"Marty's not thinking straight," Alex muttered, pacing. "We've gotta stop him from making the biggest mistake of his life! He's probably out there lost — cold, confused. Poor little guy!"

Melman nodded frantically. "But what can we do?" he moaned.

Alex stopped short. He stood there, majestic and powerful. Suddenly, he knew what to do. It was time for him to start behaving like a lion.

"We gotta go after him!" he said.

Seventeen blocks south of the zoo, Marty was trotting briskly along. His hooves clip-clopped on the pavement. He had never felt so terrific in his life.

As he passed Rockefeller Center, he noticed the multicolored international flags fluttering in the breeze.

Curious, he trotted down the walkway, past a statue of Atlas holding up the world and down to the ice skating rink.

Marty frowned. What was that white stuff?

He trotted down the stairs and sniffed at it. Then he licked it.

Cold! It was cold . . . just like ice cream.

Marty put one hoof out on it, then a second, third, and fourth. He began slipping along the ice. It was fun! Soon, he was skating around, twirling and leaping. Wee-hah! This stuff was amazing! This stuff was spectacular! This stuff was —

Hard! Marty, his legs out of control, crashed onto the ice, spinning around on his tail.

Gotta practice those moves a little more, he thought to himself. . . .

*   *   *

In the meantime, Alex, Melman, and Gloria were busy escaping from the zoo, on their way to find Marty.

Alex hung over the zoo's tall brick wall, his paws wrapped around Melman's neck. With a graceful leap, he let go, and landed on the grass.

He was free.

Melman stood there. "How am I gonna get out?" he asked.

Gloria squinted at the two-foot-thick brick wall.

"Like this," she said simply. Then she crashed through it.

There were advantages to being a hippopotamus.

"Melman," she said over her shoulder. "Come on!"

Melman hesitated.

"You know, maybe someone should stay here in case Marty comes back —" he began.

Gloria glared at him. "No way," she said firmly. "This is an *intervention*, Melman. We all gotta go!"

Alex scratched his head. "What's the fastest way to Grand Central?" he asked.

"You should take Madison," Melman said.

"Melman?" Gloria said, planting her feet in the dirt.

"Okay, okay!" Melman stepped delicately over the broken bricks. "We . . . *We* should take Madison!"

"What about Park Avenue?" Alex asked as they began to walk out of Central Park.

"Naw, Park goes two ways," Melman said authoritatively. "You can't time the lights. . . ."

Fifteen minutes later, the three friends were standing on a deserted subway platform.

"I knew we should have taken Park," Alex said to Gloria. "Are you sure this is the fastest way to Grand Central?"

Gloria shrugged. "I don't know. That's what Melman said. . . ."

Melman pulled his head out of the men's bathroom. "Hey, you guys," he said cheerfully. "They have little sinks in there where you can wash up and everything —"

Alex glared at Melman. "This isn't a field trip, Melman! This is an urgent mission to save Marty from throwing his life away. Now, where's the train?"

Melman stuck his long neck out over the tracks and looked north.

The sound of a subway train could be heard rattling down the tracks.

"Here it comes," he said, yanking his head back in just in time.

Gloria and Alex hardly noticed.

"What did Marty say to you?" she was asking Alex. "I asked you to talk to him!"

"I did, I did!" Alex snapped. "He said, 'Let's go.' Then I said, 'What, are you crazy?' Then he says, 'I'm ten years old' . . . and he has, uh, black with white stripes —"

The subway train ground to a halt, and the doors opened. Alex, Gloria, and Melman walked on. Almost everyone on the train took one look at them and ran out of the train, screaming.

While Alex, Gloria, and Melman were riding the 6 downtown, Marty was standing nose to nose with a police horse in the middle of Times Square.

Around him, shimmering red, gold, green, and blue lights flashed. Lit-up billboards advertised everything from movies and TV shows to toothpaste and hair gel.

"What ya gotta do is go straight back down West Forty-Second," the police horse was telling Marty.

"Yeah, yeah, uh-huh," Marty nodded.

"It's on your left, just past Vanderbilt," the police horse went on. "If you hit the Chrysler building, you've gone too far."

"Gee, thanks a lot, officer," Marty said. He started to cross Broadway. Cars screeched to a halt.

"Hey!" the horse yelled. "Wait for the light!"

"Sorry, sir," Marty said, hopping back up onto the curb. He pressed the crosswalk button, and the light changed from "Don't Walk" to "Walk." Marty crossed Broadway and headed east.

"Freak," muttered the police horse.

On his back, an astonished police officer was talking into his radio.

"Uh, did not copy," the radio squawked. "Did you just say 'zebra'?"

"Yup," the officer responded. "A zebra. Right in front of me. Can I shoot it?"

The radio crackled. "Negative."

"Then I'm going to need some backup," the officer said, watching the hindquarters of the zebra disappear down Forty-Second Street.

CHAPTER FOUR

As the number 6 train hurtled south, one lone, terrified passenger crouched behind his newspaper as Alex, Gloria, and Melman stared at the back page.

"Aw. The Knicks lost again!" Alex groaned.

All the man saw were Alex's teeth. *Maybe it was a mugger in a lion suit,* he thought, trembling slightly. Although it certainly *smelled* like a lion. . . .

Melman shook his head. "Whaddaya gonna do?" he shrugged. "The Knicks haven't had a championship season since, I don't know. Sometime in the eighties?"

The frightened man held out his wallet to Alex. Maybe that would make him go away.

Alex flipped it open. "Cute kids," he said to the man.

All the man heard was a roar. His teeth rattled.

Gloria glanced over at the pictures and rolled her eyes.

"You call those cute?" she muttered.

Alex gave her a dirty look as he tossed the wallet back at the man. "What was I supposed to say?" he hissed. "I didn't want to insult the guy —"

The train announcer's voice came up over the loudspeaker. "Grannnnd Cennnntrallll Staaashun!"

Alex frowned. "Did that just say 'Grand Central Station' or 'Cherokee Nation'?"

"This is it!" Gloria said excitedly.

Alex pushed the subway doors open before giving them a chance to open automatically. The man behind the newspaper fainted.

Alex and Gloria raced out of the car. Alex tossed some coins to a guy playing the drums on the subway platform.

Melman was the last to leave the car. He carefully backed out onto the platform . . . just as the doors closed on his neck.

"Ow-ow-ow-ow-ow!" he yelled, pulling as the train car started to move.

Melman finally managed to pull his head free of the car just before the train left the station. He went tumbling down the subway platform, smashing his back feet through the drummer's drums. (That was fine with the drummer, who had already decided to give up music and take that job down on Wall Street that his father had offered him.)

Melman clomped off after Alex and Gloria, his front feet still encased in two tissue boxes, his rear feet wearing the drums. "Hey, wait for me!" he called.

Alex was already bounding up the escalator, scattering horrified travelers as he went. "Move aside, people!" he cried. "We've got an emergency situation here!"

People tripped over each other as they tried to get away.

Alex jumped onto the handrail and galloped up to the top. "Hey, nobody panic," he added as people raced, screaming, for the exits. "It's not that much of an emergency. . . ."

A little old lady near the top of the escalator stepped off and beaned him on the head with her purse.

"Ow, lady!" Alex said. "Ow! Would you please —"

The lady took a can of Mace out of her purse and sprayed it in Alex's face. His eyes teared, and he rubbed at them with his paws.

"How do you like *that*?" the lady cackled.

"Argh!" Alex sniffed. "Lady, what is *wrong* with you? Get a grip on yourself!"

The lady popped Alex one more time over the head with her purse for good measure.

"Bad kitty!" she said.

Behind Alex, Gloria was wedged into the escalator. Across from her, Melman was desperately scrambling up the down escalator, trying to make it to the top. With his feet encased in both tissue boxes and drums, this wasn't easy.

Meanwhile, not too far away, Marty's hooves clip-clopped on the marble floor of Grand Central Station.

He looked up at the beautiful blue domed ceiling, covered with twinkling stars. The hall was huge and almost empty at this time of night. His hoofbeats echoed in the silence.

The few people that were there, headed to night-shift jobs or on their way home after a long day at work, stood with their mouths open, staring at the zebra in their midst.

Marty was impressed. "It sure is Grand . . . and it's Central!" he said happily.

He walked over to the ticket window and looked up at the information board.

"Dag nabbit," he muttered. "I missed the Express. Looks like I'm going to have to take the Stamford local —"

"I've got him! I've got him!"

Alex slammed into Marty, sending both of them skidding across the slippery marble floor.

"He's got him! He's got him!" Gloria shrieked, coming up behind them.

Melman heard Gloria yell just as he got to the top of the escalator. Distracted, he tripped on the last step and went flying across the marble floor. He zigged and zagged off walls like a ping-pong ball and then skidded towards the giant clock sitting atop the Information Desk.

Melman shrieked as he slammed into the clock, ripping it off its stand and ending up with it stuck on his head, covering his eyes. Blinded, he staggered around, trying to shake the clock off.

"I'm okay, I'm okay," he yelled.

"Melman?" Marty said.

"Marty?" he said.

Melman stopped short. Marty's voice was coming from somewhere off to his left. He moved towards it.

"Marty?" he called. "Is that you?"

Marty looked at Alex, Gloria, and Melman. "What are you guys doing here?" he asked.

"We're here to bring you home!" Melman explained.

"And I'm so glad we found you!" Alex roared.

"We were so worried about you," Gloria added.

Alex wrapped his legs around Marty and gave him a big hug.

"Alex, quit it," Marty said. "Look at me. I'm fine!"

Alex reluctantly released Marty

"You're fine? Oh, he's *fine*." Alex was suddenly furious. He turned to Gloria. "Did you hear that? Marty's fine. That's good to know, 'cause I was wondering . . ." He turned back to Marty. "How could you do this to us, Marty?" he screamed. "I thought we were friends!"

Marty swallowed. "What's the big deal? I was coming back in the morning. . . ."

Alex reached out, grabbed hold of Marty, and shook him until his teeth rattled. "Don't you ever . . . do . . . it . . . again. Do you realize what you put us through?"

In the distance, police sirens could be heard. Melman, still with his head stuck in the clock, turned towards the sound.

"Guys? We're running out of time," he began.

Alex turned towards him, for the first time noticing the clock on his head. "You broke the clock!" he said, horrified.

"Here . . . let me," Gloria said. She grabbed hold of the clock and started to pull . . . hard . . . just as a horde of New York City's Finest — police officers, that is — flooded into the hall in full riot gear, complete with helmets, shields, and nightsticks.

Over by a newspaper kiosk, Skipper and his band of penguins were hiding behind a paper. The tunnel they had dug to Marty's enclosure was only one of five they'd been working on for months now. One of the others had let them out right near the train station.

When the Skipper saw the police, he dropped the paper and raised his flippers. The other penguins did the same.

"We've been ratted out, boys," Skipper growled. "The law is here. Just behave like you usually do. Cute and cuddly, boys . . . cute and cuddly."

But the police weren't interested in a bunch of penguins. They had bigger fish — or rather, mammals — to fry.

They headed towards Alex, Marty, Gloria, and Melman and surrounded them.

"It's the man!" Marty hissed. Then he turned and faced the mass of men in blue, who were nervously holding up their shields.

"Good evening, officers," he began.

Alex pushed Marty out of the way. "I'll handle this," he said. "You just don't move. And don't say anything. Shhhh!"

He stepped forward. The police officers stared at him in shock. After all, it isn't every day that you're confronted with a lion in Grand Central Station.

"Hey, how ya doin'?" Alex began, trying to lighten the mood. "You know what? Everything's cool. We just had a little situation here . . . a little internal situation. Actually, my friend here —" he gestured to Marty. "My friend went a little bit crazy. A little cuckoo in the head. Happens to everybody. This city gets to us all —"

Marty bristled. "Hey. Don't call me cuckoo!" he said.

Alex turned and glared at him. "Just . . . shhhh! I will handle this!" he hissed.

He turned back to face a trembling animal control officer. The officer was carrying a dart gun.

Just then, the little old lady who had hit Alex before darted over to him again and gave him one more whack with her purse. "I got him!" she said proudly.

A couple of valiant police officers raced in and grabbed her, dragging her away.

Alex rubbed his head. "Would you give a guy a break?" he moaned.

He turned back to the police. "We're just gonna take my friend home," he went on soothingly, "and forget this whole thing ever happened. Right? No harm, no foul. . . ."

Alex took a step forward. The officers all took a step back.

Alex frowned. "Hey. It's cool. I'm Alex. Alex the lion? From the zoo?"

The officers took another step back.

Alex turned to Marty. "What's wrong with them?" he asked. "Why are they acting this way?"

The animal control officer shot a tranquilizer dart into Alex's haunch.

Alex staggered a bit on his feet.

"Hey," he said, slowly sinking to his knees. "I feel really . . . good. . . ."

Then everything went black.

CHAPTER FIVE

"Al-ex! Al-ex! Al-ex!!"

Alex opened his eyes. He was in a large wooden crate at the entrance to the zoo.

People around him were screaming and shouting his name. Reporters scrambled as cameras alternately focused on them and on the crate.

A nearby reporter spoke into her microphone.

"Last night's incident in Grand Central is what animal rights activists have been shouting about for years," she said. "The animals clearly don't want to be in captivity. Now they will be sent back to their natural habitat, where they will live the rest of their lives in the freedom they so clearly desire."

Alex groaned. His head was splitting.

"Hey, a little help here," he began.

"He's awake! He's awake!" a few people screamed.

About twenty-five tranquilizer darts hit Alex at the same time.

Then everything went black again.

When Alex awoke, he couldn't see a thing.

"Ugh. Oh, my head," he moaned, rubbing his eyes with his paws.

He groggily got to his feet. But before he could take two steps, he found himself up against an obstruction of some sort.

He felt his way around . . . and then he panicked.

"Ahhhh! A box! A box! I'm in a box! They're transferring me to another zoo! But they can't! They can't transfer me . . . not me, not Alex!"

He clawed at the sides of the crate, terrified. "I can't breathe! I can't breathe! Darkness creeping in . . . can't breathe! Walls closing in around me!"

Alex held himself and started to rock back and forth.

"So alone. I'm so alone," he moaned.

Suddenly, two eyes appeared in the dark next to him.

"Alex? Are you there?"

It was Marty's voice.

"Marty?" Alex yelled.

"Yeah. Talk to me, buddy!"

Alex felt a wave of relief roll through him. "Marty! You're here!" he said.

"What's going on?" Marty asked. "Are you okay?"

Alex took a deep breath. "Yeah, I'm fine," he said. "But this doesn't look good, Marty."

"Alex? Marty? Is that you?"

Gloria's voice drifted up from a crate below them.

Alex sat up. "Gloria! You're here too?"

Marty blinked. "Gloria? I am *loving* the sound of your voice!"

Gloria looked around her box. "What is going on here?" she asked.

"We're all in crates," Alex told her.

"Oh, dear," Gloria said sadly.

"Sleeping just knocks me out," a fourth voice said just to her left.

"Is that Melman?" Marty asked.

"Melman!" Alex cried, overjoyed.

"Melman," Gloria said. "Are you okay?"

"Yeah. No, I'm fine," Melman said, stretching his neck. "I often doze off when I'm getting an MRI."

"Melman, you're not getting an MRI," Alex said.

"Catscan?" Melman asked hopefully.

"No, no catscan," Alex said. "It's a transfer. A zoo transfer!"

Melman's eyes opened wide. "Zoo transfer?" he gasped. "Oh, no! No, no! I can't be transferred. I have an appointment with Dr. Goldberg at five. There are prescriptions that have to be filled. No other zoo could afford my medical care! And I am NOT going HMO —"

Melman's voice rose to a tortured squeak.

"Melman! Calm down, Melman!" Gloria called.

Marty nodded. "Take it easy, Melman," he said, with more confidence than he felt. "We are going to be okay. That's Oh-Kizzay!"

"No, we are *not* going to be oh-kizzay!" Alex snapped. "Now, because of you, we're screwed!"

Marty's eyes narrowed. "Because of *me*? I fail to see how this is my fault —"

"You're kidding, right, Marty?" Gloria's voice was icy.

Alex gritted his teeth. "You! You made the people mad! You bit the hand, Marty. You bit the hand! 'I don't know who I am! I don't know who I am! I've got to go find myself in the wild!' Oh, please!"

"I didn't ask you to come after me, did I?" Marty said defensively.

"He does have a point," Melman began.

"WHAT?" Alex shrieked.

Melman shrugged. "I did say we should stay at the zoo, but you guys —"

Alex growled softly. "Melman, just shut it. You're the one that suggested the whole idea to him in the first place!"

"Alex." Gloria's voice was stern. "Leave Melman out of this, please."

"Thank you, Gloria," Melman said. "Yeah, Alex. It's not my fault we were transferred —"

"Shut it, Melman," Gloria said. "I feel sick to my stomach. Does anyone else feel sick?"

"I feel sick," Melman said helpfully.

"You *always* feel sick," Alex muttered.

* * *

Somewhere else on the cargo ship — for that's where Alex, Marty, Gloria, and Melman were, along with scores of other animals being transported back to the wild — Kowalski the penguin stuck his head out of his crate and looked around.

"Progress report!" Skipper barked behind him.

Kowalski stared at the writing on his crate. "It's an older code, Skipper," he said. "I can't make it out."

Skipper stuck his head out of the crate and looked around.

A few crates over, some monkeys chattered amongst themselves.

"Hey, higher mammal!" Skipper called over to them. "Can you read?"

Mason the chimpanzee looked out. "No," he said. "Phil can read, though. Some zoologist lady taught him sign language. Phil? Come on out, you filthy monkey!"

Phil stuck his head out of his crate. He stared at the writing on it. Then he began to sign.

Mason watched him, translating. "Hmm? Yes. Ship to Kenya Wildlife Preserve. Africa."

"Africa?" Skipper frowned. "For us penguins? That ain't gonna fly!" He looked around. "Rico!" he called.

Rico stuck his head out of the crate. Coughing up a paper clip, he expertly picked the lock.

In five seconds, the penguins were free.

Five minutes later, up on the bridge, the captain was listening to Bob Marley on his headphones when a penguin came up behind him and gave him a karate chop to the neck.

The captain fell forward, out cold.

The penguins were in control of the ship.

"I was the star in the greatest city on Earth!" Alex was growling. "A *king*! Loved by my people! And you've ruined everything!"

He threw his weight against the side of his crate, knocking Marty backwards.

"Guys! Guys, listen. Let's just be civil —" Gloria began.

"Loved by your people?" Marty shot back. "If the people loved you, it's only because they didn't know the real you!"

He slammed against his own crate, sending it crashing into Alex's and making Gloria and Melman's crates shudder.

"Guys? You both quit it right now!" Gloria said sternly. "Don't make me come up there. I'll get to whoopin' on both you all."

But the lion and the zebra wouldn't listen.

CRASH! Alex slammed against his crate.

BAM! Marty crashed against his.

"I thought I knew the real you," Alex said grimly. "And Marty? Your black and white stripes? They cancel each other out. You're NOTHING!"

CRASH!

BAM!

The ropes that secured the crates to the deck of the ship began to fray. . . .

"Stop it!" Melman screamed. "Stop it! Stop it!"

Gloria groaned. "You are not helping the situation, Melman," she said.

CRASH!

BAM!

The ropes snapped . . . and Marty's crate went skidding across the deck.

Back on the bridge, Private the penguin was randomly punching buttons on the shipboard computer. The screen read, "ACCESS DENIED."

"Status?" barked Skipper.

Private shook his head. "It's no good, Skipper," he said. "I don't know the codes."

"Don't give me excuses, Private!" Skipper hollered. "Give me results!" He turned to Rico. "Navigation!"

Rico gestured to a huge map. It was of the African coast. The ship's current position was marked — in the Mozambique Channel, just off the island of Madagascar.

Of course, this was no help to Rico. He couldn't read a map, and even if he could read it, he had never heard of the Mozambique Channel or Madagascar.

Suddenly, Private turned to Skipper.

"I did it! he yelled. "We're in!"

The computer screen now read, "Override Accepted."

Skipper nodded. "Then let's get this tin can turned around," he said crisply. He turned to look at his crew. "You . . . you . . . and you."

The three penguins jumped on the ship's wheel and started to turn it.

The ship made a sharp turn to starboard.

Up on the deck, the three crates carrying Alex, Melman and Gloria were thrown free. They flew across the deck.

One by one, they piled up against Marty's crate, which was jammed against the chain railing at the edge. *Smack . . . smack . . . SMACK!*

The last crate to hit was Gloria's. And when the two-ton-hippopotamus-filled crate hit the others, the chain railing snapped.

All four crates plunged into the sea.

CHAPTER SIX

As the ship sailed away, the four crates bobbed in the ocean, moving up and down with the swells.

Alex peered out of an air hole. He watched as the ship disappeared over the horizon.

"Guys?" he yelled, trying to find his friends. But the vast expanse of ocean — at least the expanse he could see from his tiny peephole — was empty.

"Oh, no!" he cried. "Marty? Gloria? Melman?"

"Alex!" Marty's voice came back at him.

"Marty!" Alex called gratefully.

"Alex!"

"Marty!"

"Hold it! Abuhbuhbuh. . . ."

"Marty?"

In Marty's crate, water was seeping in between the cracks. He had all four hooves covering four leaking holes, and was covering a fifth with his tongue. He pulled his tongue off the hole for a second.

"Just a minute," he called out to Alex. "I'm a little bit busy right now . . ."

He put his tongue back on the fifth hole again.

Alex panicked. "Marty! No, wait! Come back! Marty!"

But Marty didn't answer. He was too busy trying to keep his crate from filling up with water.

Alex moaned. "Don't go, Marty," he whispered. "Don't go!"

He peered out of the hole in his crate.

But all he could see was the sea.

Marty was gone.

Alex's crate floated atop the ocean for what seemed like days.

For the most part, he stared out of the air hole, desperately hoping to see one of his friends.

But there was nothing out there.

Alex was catching a quick cat-nap when suddenly, his crate rolled over and over again and smashed down onto something.

"Huh?" Alex said, startled out of a dream of a rare T-bone steak . . .

The crate had smashed open. Alex found himself washed up on a beautiful white beach.

He spat out a mouthful of sand and wiped his tongue with his paw.

Then he shook his head and looked up . . . and screamed.

"Aaaaagh!"

In front of him was a wall of dense tropical jungle.

Alex's heart began to pound. He was alone . . . in the wild!!

He turned and looked across the expanse of beach.

"Marty! Melman! Gloria!" he called. "Hey, anyone! Hello? Marty? Melman? Gloria! Aaagh!"

Alex raced across the sand, desperately looking for his friends.

Seven hours later, he was still looking. His mane was tangled and matted from the salt water. He was an exhausted mess.

"Marty, Melman, Gloria, Gloria, Melman, Marty, Marty, Gelman, Marty, Glormy, Glormy, Melman —" he groaned.

He collapsed in a heap, and was about to pass out when he heard a voice.

"Help! Whoa! Hey . . . whoa! Get me out of this thing! Somebody? Hello? Get me out of this thing! Hello, somebody?"

Alex picked his head up off the sand. Was that . . . Melman?

Alex headed in the direction of the voice. He hopped onto some rocks . . . and there, just down the beach, was a tall crate, with four long legs running back and forth.

"Melman!" Alex cried. He raced after the crate. "Melman! Hang on!"

Melman's crate fell over. Alex ripped the top off and tried to pull Melman out by his horns.

"I gotcha, buddy!" he said excitedly.

"Ow-ow-ow-ow-ow-ow-ow-ow-ow-ow-ow-ow!" Melman yelped. "The horns! Ix-nay on the orsn-hay!"

Alex pulled some more, but it wasn't working. He looked around for something to use to pry Melman out of his crate.

Near the edge of the jungle was a log.

"Wait a second, Melman," Alex told his friend, racing away. "Wait right there!"

"What are you doing?" Melman asked worriedly.

"I'm getting you outta the box!" Alex called, grabbing hold of the log. "Relax!"

"Alex?" Melman asked, craning his neck around to try to see what Alex was doing.

Alex came back into sight, dragging the log. "Just close your eyes and say your prayers," he said cheerfully. "Here goes nothing. Hold still!"

Melman panicked.

"Alex, what are you doing? Wait! Wait! Wait! No, come on, wait! Don't hit me with that thing! Wait! Wait —"

He cast his eyes around desperately as Alex raised the huge log over his head.

"Hey, it's Gloria! Hey, wait, wait, it's Gloria!" Melman shrieked suddenly. Of course, it wasn't Gloria. He just wanted to stop this crazy lion from hitting him with the giant stick —

That very second, a large crate marked "Hippo" washed up on the beach.

Alex turned, the log inches from Melman's crate.

Melman's eyes opened wider.

"Hey, it *is* Gloria," he gasped, just before he passed out.

"Gloria!"

Alex dropped the log and raced over to Gloria's crate. "Gloria?" he called. "Are you in there?"

Gloria kicked open her crate, sending Alex flying through the air. He landed on Melman's crate, breaking it apart.

Gloria stepped out from the wreckage.

"Alex!" she cried.

"Gloria!" Alex yelled back.

"Alex? Gloria?" Melman moaned.

"Whoaaaa!"

Alex, Gloria, and Melman turned towards the shore.

There, surfing towards land on the back of two dolphins, was Marty.

"Yeah, right. Now, left. No, no — your left! Right here's good —"

The dolphins neatly deposited Marty on the beach a few yards away from Alex.

"Sorry, guys," he said to the dolphins. "I don't have any money on me right now. I'll have to get you later."

Marty turned to face his friends.

Alex beamed.

"Marty!" he said, racing towards his friend.

"Alex!" Marty grinned and started to race towards Alex.

But then Alex's expression changed. He bared his teeth.

"Marty! I'm going to KILL you!" he snarled, still racing towards his friend.

Marty skidded to a halt, turned, and raced in the opposite direction.

"Don't you run away from me!" Alex's voice dropped an octave as he chased Marty up and down the beach. "Come here!"

"Hey, hold up!" Marty gasped. "Whoa! Wait a second. Calm down! I gotta tell you something. Calm down. Calm down."

Gloria and Melman ran up from behind just as Alex overtook Marty. They jumped onto Alex just as Alex grabbed Marty, and all four of them fell in a heap on the beach.

Melman suddenly hugged Marty. "Marty!" he said, blubbering. "I'm so glad you're here!"

"Look at us!" Gloria added, sniffing. "We're all together, safe and sound."

"Yeah," Melman said. He stopped and looked around. "Uh . . . where exactly is here?"

The four animals turned. Behind them was the massive wall of tropical jungle, brilliantly lit by the morning sun.

Melman blinked. "San Diego," he decided.

Gloria turned to him. "San Diego?" she said in disbelief.

"White sandy beaches. Cleverly simulated natural environment. Wide-open enclosures." Melman nodded. "I'm telling you, this could be the San Diego Zoo. Complete with fake rocks." He tapped a rock. "Wow, that really feels real!"

Alex started to pace. "San Diego?" he groaned. "What could be worse than San Diego?"

"I don't know," Marty said. "This place is crack-a-lackin'!" I could hang here. . . ."

Alex turned to Marty.

"I'm gonna kill you, Marty!" he shrieked. "I'm gonna strangle you and burn you and dig you up and clone you and kill all your clones!"

Marty backed away. "Wait, wait, wait! Take it easy, Alex. Calm down! Don't get outta control. Twenty second time out!"

"STOP IT!"

Gloria pushed her massive bulk between Alex and Marty.

She grabbed Alex by the shoulders and held on tight.

"We're just going to find the people, get checked in, and have this mess straightened out," she said authoritatively.

Alex shook his head back and forth. "Oh, great," he moaned. "This is just great. San Diego! Now I'll have to compete with Shamu and his smug little grin. I can't top that! I'm ruined! I'm done! I'm outta the business!" He turned on Marty. "And it's your fault, Marty. You've ruined me!!!"

Marty's eyes widened. "C'mon, Alex," he said. "Do you honestly think I intended all of this to happen? You want me to say I'm sorry? Is that what you want? Okay. I'm —"

"Shhhh."

Alex's ears flicked up and back. He held his paw up.

Marty turned to Gloria, insulted. "Alex just shushed me!"

Gloria sighed. "Look, Marty. You've got to be just a little more under-standing about —"

"Shhhh!"

This time, Alex waved his paw at Gloria.

Gloria set her shoulders. "Don't you shush me!" she began.

Alex shook his head. "Be quiet! Don't you hear that?" he hissed.

The four friends picked up their heads and listened.

Drifting over the jungle treetops were the faint strains of . . . could it be? Music?

Minutes later, Alex, Marty, Melman, and Gloria were racing through the jungle towards the music.

"I hear it now!" Marty crowed.

"Where there's music, there's people!" Gloria panted.

"We'll go right to the head honcho," Alex decided.

"A sidewalk would be nice," Melman said, stepping into a hole. "Ouch!"

"Yeah. What a dump," Gloria agreed.

Alex rolled his eyes. "They should call it the San De Lame-o Zoo. First they tell you, 'Hey we've got this great open plain thing. Let the animals run wild.' Next thing ya know . . . it's flowers in your hair and everyone's huggin' everybody. . . ."

Melman caught his neck on a vine. "Ouchy ouch ouch!" he said.

Marty bent back a branch to clear a path for the others. "I don't know," he said. "This place kind of grows on you. This way, guys. Come on!"

The music was getting louder and louder. Marty let go of the branch. It snapped back, hitting Alex in the face. He flipped over, hitting a rock and catching a thorn in his paw.

"Agh!" he yelped.

He bounced up onto three legs and hopped into a giant spider web.

"Ack! Ick!" He desperately tried to wipe the gooey web off his mane. As he did, he knocked into a tree and tripped over a log.

The tree fell on him.

Marty, Melman, and Gloria saw none of this. They were further ahead, racing towards the source of the music — a giant, twisted, lit-up baobob tree that towered over the jungle like a strange monument.

"Okay, let's make a good impression on the people," Gloria said, skidding to a halt. "Smiles, everyone." She turned to Melman. "Is that the best you can do?"

"I'm not smiling," Melman grunted. "I've got gas."

Gloria sighed. "It'll have to do."

She turned and pulled back some leaves and vines. She, Melman, and Marty peered cautiously into the clearing.

Large, writhing shadows danced across a backdrop of leaves, vines, and brightly-colored tropical flowers. But the shadows weren't made by people. They were made by a troop of small mouse-like lemurs, dancing to the jungle beat.

Gloria's mouth dropped open. "It's not people!" she said. "It's *animals!*"

"California animals," Melman said disapprovingly.

"Wow," Marty breathed. "This is like . . . like a party!"

One of the lemurs — clearly a head honcho — leapt into the middle of the clearing and began to sing and dance to the beat.

"What kind of a zoo *is* this?" Gloria gasped.

"I just saw twenty-six blatant health code violations," Melman clucked disapprovingly. "No . . . twenty-seven!"

Marty just stared.

"I'm likin' San Diego," he said, swaying slightly as the music took him. This place is fresh!" He wiggled his tail. "Come on, you guys. I brought my hips! Let's dance!"

He started to head out into the clearing. But Gloria held him back.

"Wait a minute," she said. "Where's Alex?"

The three friends turned and peered behind them. Alex was nowhere in sight.

"I don't know," Marty shrugged. "But he's missing one heck of a party!"

Suddenly, the music stopped.

"The fossa! The fossa are attacking! Run for your lives!" a lemur screamed.

Four menacing fossa — about forty-five pounds of nasty weasel muscle — entered the clearing, carrying primitive knives and forks.

The lemurs fled into the bushes.

Alex appeared behind Gloria, brushing spider web out of his nose.

"Ewwww, I hate spider webs," he said. "Thanks for waiting up, guys ..."

He parted the curtain of foliage and peered out into the clearing.

It was empty — except for the four fossa, who were busy tossing a tiny lemur named Mort in a salad bowl.

Clearly, Mort was lunch.

Alex stepped out. "Hey," he said to the fossa. "Um, we just got in from New York and we're looking for a zoo supervisor because we've been sitting for hours on that beach back there and nobody's even bothered to show up. I don't know how things are, uh ... yeah, I don't know how things are normally run around here, but obviously there's been some kind of major screw-up, which is cool, so if you could just point us toward the administrative offices, we'll just —"

A large, hairy spider appeared on Alex's shoulder.

"Well, howdy do," it said politely.

If Alex hated spiderwebs, it was nothing to how much he hated spiders.

"AAAAAAGH!!!!" he screamed.

Then he proceeded to go nuts.

He jumped five feet into the air, twisting and turning, growling and snarling.

The fossa looked up from their prospective meal in terror. They had never seen anything like Alex flipping out, and it was a terrible sight.

They dropped Mort into the salad bowl, dropped the salad bowl on the ground, and ran back into the jungle.

In a bush nearby, the lemur king's eyes opened wide.

"Did you see that, Maurice?" he whispered to his chief bodyguard.

"Yes, King Julien." Maurice nodded. "He scared the fossa away!"

In the meantime, Gloria had picked up a branch and was whacking away at Alex and the ground around him, trying to kill the poor spider (who, as he shakily told his wife and three thousand children later that evening at dinner, was only trying to be friendly!)

"C'mon, Gloria! Get it! Get it! Smack it good!" Marty and Melman shouted.

"That's right!" the spider called from a safe distance away as Gloria continued to beat poor Alex! "Get it! Smack it!"

Then it skittered away in the tall grass.

The lemurs stared out from the surrounding bushes as the strange, giant animals went crazy.

"King Julien!" little Mort gasped. "What are they? What are they?"

King Julien rubbed his chin. "They are aliens," he finally decided. "Savage aliens from the savage future."

"They have come to kill us and take our precious metals!" babbled Maurice.

Mort fainted dead away.

King Julien looked down at the little lemur.

"Get up, Mort," he hissed. "Don't be near the king's feet, okay? We're in the bushes. We're hiding. Shhh. Be quiet everyone, including me. Shhhh." King Julien looked around. "Who is making that noise?"

Maurice stared at him.

"Oh. It's me again." King Julien nodded.

In the clearing, Gloria was still beating at Alex with the stick.

"Stop it!" Alex hollered. "Enough! Enough with the stick."

Gloria tossed the stick aside and helped Alex up.

"Is it still on me?" Alex asked, craning his neck to see his back. "Ewww, I hate spiders."

Melman peered at Alex.

"She got it," he told Alex. "I think she got it. . . ."

Gloria nodded. "It's okay. It's gone."

In the bushes, Mort was staring at Alex in horror.

"They are savages!" he squeaked. "Tonight, we die!" And he fell at King Julien's feet.

King Julien stared down at him. "The feet! I told you about . . . I told you . . . I told every . . . my feet!" The King looked around at his subjects. "Didn't I tell him about my feet?"

Mort popped up again.

King Julien scratched his head. "Wait!"

The lemurs all waited.

"I have a plan," King Julien went on.

"Really?" Maurice just stared at him.

King Julien looked down his nose at Maurice. "I have devised a cunning test to see whether these are savage killers."

Then he smiled at poor little Mort, pulled his foot back, and kicked the little lemur out of the bushes.

"If they eat Mort, we will know," he said wisely to Maurice.

Maurice just rolled his eyes.

Mort landed at Alex's feet.

The four friends looked down. Then Marty took a step forward.

"Hi, there!" he said cheerfully.

Alex waved a paw.

"Ah, let me handle it," he said, stepping in front of Marty. "Alex handles it. Marty does *nothing*."

Alex bent down and addressed Mort.

"Hiiiiiii theeeeeeerrrrreeeeee," he purred.

Mort, staring up at Alex's sharp teeth, began to cry.

Melman frowned. "Oh, Alex. What did you do?"

Alex blushed.

"Oh, gee, shhhhh!" he said to Mort. "No, no, no, stop. It's okay. I'm just a silly lion. Oh, gee. . . ."

Mort cried even louder.

Marty, Gloria, and Melman hurried to comfort Mort.

"Poor little baby!" Gloria crooned. "Did that big mean lion scare you?"

Mort nodded a tiny lemur nod.

"He did?" Gloria said gently. "He's a big bad ol' putty tat, isn't he? Come on. Mama will hold you."

Gloria picked Mort up and hugged him gently. Mort cooed.

Melman peered over her shoulder. "They are so cute from a reasonable distance," he said.

Gloria tickled Mort, who giggled. "Awww, just look at you!" She smiled. "Aren't you just the sweetest little thing? I just want to dunk you in my coffee. . . ."

From the bushes, King Julien stared out in disbelief.

"They're just a bunch of sissies!" he said.

"I don't know." Maurice stared at Alex. "There is still something about the one with the crazy hairdo that I find suspicious."

"Oh, nonsense, Maurice," said King Julien authoritatively. He turned to his subjects. "Come on, everyone! Let's go out and meet the sissies!"

From all the bushes around the clearing came small cheers. Then hundreds of tiny lemurs raced out to surround Alex, Marty, Gloria, and Melman.

Maurice jumped up on a nearby rock and cleared his throat.

"Presenting Your Royal Highness, our illustrious King Julien the 13th, self-proclaimed Lord of the Lemurs. Everybody cheer."

The lemurs all cheered.

Then King Julien stepped from his hiding place.

Marty stared at him. "He's got style," he said grudgingly.

"What is he?" Alex whispered. "A guinea pig?"

"I think he's a squirrel," Melman said.

King Julien hopped on the shoulders of another lemur, who hopped on the shoulders of another, who hopped on the shoulders of another. When he was tall enough to meet Marty's eyes, he spoke.

"Welcome, giant sissies," he said regally. "Please feel free to bask in my glow."

Alex nodded. "Definitely a squirrel," he agreed.

"We thank you with enormous gratitude for chasing away the fossa," King Julien went on.

"The whatsa?" Gloria asked.

"The fossa," Julien explained. "They are always annoying us by trespassing, interrupting our parties and ripping our limbs off —"

"Yeah, that's nice," Alex interrupted. "Look, hey, we just want to find out where the people are, so if you could —"

A DAY at the ZOO

ALEX the LION

MARTY the ZEBRA

GLORIA the HIPPO

MELMAN the GIRAFFE

the PENGUINS

the LEMURS

WELCOME to the WILD

Maurice stared at Alex. "Oh, my," he said. "What big teeth you have!"

King Julien tsk-tsked. "Shame on you, Maurice!" he said. "Do you now see that you have insulted the freak?" He turned to Alex. "His rudeness will not go unpunished."

"But first," he went on, "you must tell me . . . who the heck are you?"

Alex stepped forward. "I am Alex. *The* Alex. And this is Gloria, Marty, and Melman."

King Julien nodded. "And just where are you giants from?"

"We're from New York," Alex explained.

"Ah. All hail the New York Giants!" King Julien proclaimed.

The lemurs cheered and leaped about.

Alex frowned.

"What are they?" he muttered. "Part of some sort of inbreeding program? Well, I say we just gotta ask these bozos to tell us where the people are."

King Julien turned to Alex. "Oh, we Bozos have the people, of course."

"You do?" Melman said eagerly.

"Oh. Well, great," Alex said. "Where are they?"

King Julien pointed. "One of them is up there," he said. "Don't you just love the people? Not a very lively bunch, though. . . ."

Alex and the others looked up. A skeleton of a man in a parachute was hanging from a high tree above their heads.

Alex winced. "Do you have any *live* people?" he asked in a strangled voice.

King Julien shrugged. "Oh, no. Only dead ones."

Maurice nodded. "I mean, if we had a lot of live people here, it wouldn't be called the wild, would it?"

A big grin began to spread across Marty's face. "The wild?" he breathed.

Alex's heart skipped a beat.

"Hold up there," he said. "You mean the 'live in a mud hut, wipe yourself with a leaf' kind of wild?"

King Julien smiled and nodded.

Gloria rolled her eyes. "Oy vey!" she groaned.

"Oy vey!" King Julien echoed happily.

"Oy vey!" chorused all the lemurs, dancing around. "Oy vey!"

Alex stared at the leaping lemurs.

"Could you excuse me for just a moment?" he asked King Julien.

"Of course," King Julien replied. "Oy vey!"

CHAPTER SEVEN

Alex staggered onto the beach, crying hysterically.

"Help!" he screamed at the vast blue ocean. "Heeeeeeeeelp!"

Then he plunged into the water.

Gloria crashed through the underbrush and out onto the sand.

"What are you *doing?*" she screamed at Alex. She grabbed hold of Alex and held fast.

"Let me go! shrieked Alex. "I'm swimming back to New York! I know my chances are slim . . . but I've got to try!"

"But you can't swim!" Gloria reminded him.

"I said my chances are slim," Alex groaned.

Melman raced onto the beach, vines wrapped around his head and covering his eyes.

"Arrrrgh!" he yelled. "Nature! It's all over me! Get it off. I can't see. I can't see!"

Gloria stepped on the vines as he raced past, tearing them off.

Melman stopped short and looked around. "I can't see!" he whimpered. "But I don't wanna see!"

He buried his head in the sand.

Behind him, Marty pranced out of the jungle and onto the beach.

"We're in the wii-iild!" he sang and danced. "We're in the wii-iild!"

Gloria sighed. "Okay," she said, getting a better grip on Alex's throat. "There's obviously been a little mistake, that's all."

Melman pulled his head up and spit out some sand. "Yeah," he said. "A colossal little mistake!"

"Chill, Melman!" Gloria snapped. "I mean, relax! I'm sure the people didn't dump us here on purpose. As soon as they realize what happened, they'll come looking for us. Right?"

Alex gasped for air. "Gloria?" he wheezed.

"I'll bet they're already on their way," Gloria went on.

"You think?" Melman said wistfully. He looked out to sea.

Far, far out at sea, Skipper was at the ship's radio. Reggae music was playing. He turned the volume up.

"Well, boys," he told his excited crew. "We're headed for Antarctica! It's going to be ice-cold sushi for breakfast!"

Kowalski and Private high-fived each other.

Skipper turned to Rico. "Rico?" he asked.

Rico popped the cork on a bottle of champagne.

Back on the beach, Melman was busy writing his will in the sand. Behind him was a large trench.

"I, Melman Menkowitz, being of sound mind and unsound body, have divided my estate equally among the three of you. . . ."

A large wave washed up onto the short, destroying part of the will.

Marty bounded up. "Hey! A latrine!" he said, admiring Melman's trench. "Outdoor plumbing!"

"It's not a latrine," Alex snorted. "It's a grave. You've sent Melman to his grave! Are you happy??"

Marty shrugged. "Oh, come on," he said cheerfully. "This isn't the end. This is a whole new beginning. This could be the best thing that's ever happened to us!"

Alex's mane stood on end.

"No! No! No! No! No!" he growled. "This isn't the best thing that's ever happened to us! You abused the power of the birthday wish and brought this bad luck on us all!"

"Yeah," Melman said, nodding. "Why'd you tell us your wish? You're not supposed to do that."

"Wait a minute!" Marty protested. "You guys made me tell you! Besides, this is *good* luck! There are no fences, no schedules. This place is beautiful. Baby, we were born to be here!"

Alex wasn't listening. He was busy drawing a line in the sand, dividing the portion of the beach where Marty stood from the portion where he and the others were standing.

"Okay!" he said. "I've had enough of this!" He pointed across the line. "That is your side of the island, Marty, and this is our side of the island. Your side is the bad side, where you can prance and skip

around like a magical pixie horse and do whatever the heck you want to do all day and . . ." Words failed him. He pointed at his own feet. "This is the good side of the island, for those who love New York and care about going home."

Marty shook his head. "C'mon, Alex —" he said, trying to cross the line.

Alex stepped forward. "No! Back! Get back. Get back on your side!"

Gloria's ears quivered. "You know what?" she said. "This isn't good. We should really try to work together. This really isn't the time to point fingers." She pointed at Marty. "Even if it is all his fault."

Marty snorted. "Oh, you too, Gloria, huh? Okay. You all have your side, and I have mine. If you need me, I'll be over here, on the fun side of the island. Having a good ole time. A yabba-dabba-doo ole time."

He turned away and trotted across the sand, singing.

"That's not the fun side!" Alex screamed. "*This* is the fun side! Where we're going to have a great time surviving until we go home! Whew, I love this side! This side's the best! That side stinks."

Melman stared after Marty. "So. Now what do we do?" he asked Alex.

"Don't worry," Alex said, glaring at Marty's tail. "I have a plan to get us rescued. . . ."

"No. That's poison," Melman said to Gloria. "And that is . . . and so is that. Poison . . . poison . . . poison."

Gloria, who was busy looking for food at the edge of the jungle, picked up a rock and threw it at Melman.

"That's a rock," Melman said helpfully.

Alex, in the meantime, was picking up pieces of wood on the beach for the structure he was building out of planks and palm trunks. He stared up at it. It looked pretty good.

"I can't wait to see the look on Marty's face when he sees this," Alex muttered, looking over at Marty's half of the beach.

Marty was relaxing in his glamorous cabana, sipping something from a coconut shell. He smiled smugly as Alex glared at him.

Hours later, Alex was busy putting the finishing touches on his structure from high up on some scaffolding. Below him on the beach, Melman was rubbing two sticks together, trying to make fire.

"Ta-da!" Alex said proudly. "I defy any rescue boat within a million miles to miss this baby . . ."

Gloria stared up in admiration at what Alex had built — a thirty-foot-tall version of the Statue of Liberty, island-style.

"When the moment is right," Alex called down to her, "we will light this beacon of liberty. A great fire will result, a boat will see it, and we'll be rescued from this awful nightmare. What do you think? Pretty cool, huh?"

He looked over at Melman. "How's the liberty fire going, Melman?"

Melman glanced up. "Great," he said. "Idiot," he added, under his breath.

"I heard that," Alex said.

"What's the use," Melman asked. "I'm gonna die anyway."

"If you're going to die anyway," Alex said dryly, "you could at least spontaneously combust so the rest of us can get a fire out of the deal."

Across the beach, Marty was roasting mango marshmallows over a roaring campfire.

"Why can't we just borrow some of Marty's fire?" Melman whined.

"That's 'wild' fire," Alex snorted. "We're not using 'wild' fire on Lady Liberty. Now, rub, Melman!"

Melman started to shake. "I've been rubbing . . . I can't . . . I can't do it!" he cried, throwing the boards down onto the beach.

They burst into flame.

Melman stared at them, his eyes wide. "I made fire!" he gloated. "I made fire. I, Melman Mankowitz, made fire!"

Suddenly, Melman realized that the boards were tied to his feet . . . and they were burning!

"Aaaah!" he shrieked. "Fire! Fire! Get it off me!"

Melman raced around the beach, trying to douse the flames.

"Melman!" Gloria cried. "Hold still!"

She threw some sand at Melman, trying to put out the fire. But instead, the sand got into Melman's eyes. Blinded, the frantic giraffe

staggered around the beach. Then he slammed into Alex's Statue of Liberty . . . and set it on fire, too.

Alex was still stuck on top.

The flames licked at Lady Liberty's skirts.

"No, not yet!" Alex yelled. "I don't see a ship yet!"

"Jump, Alex, jump!" Gloria screamed. "Don't worry! Cats always land on their feet!"

Alex jumped. He landed face-first in the sand.

"Man. What kind of a cat are you, anyway?" Gloria sighed, shaking her head.

Melman jammed his sticks into the sand, putting them out. Alex stared at his burning monument in despair.

"You maniac," he groaned, sinking to his knees. "You burned it up! Darn you! Darn you all to heck!"

Melman stared wistfully over at Marty's side of the beach, where Marty was busy dancing the hula.

"Can we go over to the fun side now?" he asked wistfully.

Alex stared over at Marty's side of the beach. Marty was telling a joke. Gloria and Melman laughed loudly.

Alex turned away.

Marty noticed. He left Melman and Gloria and slowly wandered over to the line in the sand.

Alex pretended not to notice.

"Yo, Al?" Marty said. "Melman and Gloria are over there having a good time. There's room on the fun side for one more. . . ."

Alex looked down. "No, thanks," he muttered.

Marty sighed. "Alex," he said, "being here in the wild — it's like my dream come true. Look. The people are going to rescue us soon enough. In the meantime, maybe if you just gave this place a chance, I don't know, you might even . . . enjoy yourself!"

Alex shook his head. "Marty, I'm tired. I'm hungry. I just want to go home."

Marty sighed again. "Alex? Why is everything always about what you want?"

He turned and walked away. Alex slumped down on the sand. He wasn't going over to the fun side — no matter what Marty or anybody else said.

He was going to stay on this side and wait for help — if it took forever.

A few hours later, Alex crept over to Marty's side of the beach. Melman and Gloria were already there, drinking out of coconuts and playing charades.

Alex knocked on Marty's door. It was only a door, sitting in the

middle of the beach. Marty hadn't gotten around to building the walls yet.

"Who is it?" Marty called.

"It's the pizza man," Alex growled. "Who do you think it is?"

Marty went over to the "door" and stared out the peephole. "Can I help you?" he said frostily.

"Can I come over to the fun side?" Alex muttered.

Marty opened the door slightly. "I beg your pardon?"

"Can . . . I . . . come . . . to . . . the . . . fun . . . side?" Alex said slowly.

Marty opened the door wide. "Sure, Alex!" he said happily. "Welcome to Casa de Wild! Take a load off! Hey, wipe your feet!"

Alex wiped his feet on Marty's doormat, and walked through the "door."

On his side of the beach, Marty had constructed a beautiful island cabana, complete with fire pit, ceiling fan, fountain, and wet bar.

"Alex!" Gloria waved from a round bed made of sand. Nearby, Melman lounged on a sand couch.

"Mi casa es su casa," Marty said expansively.

Alex looked around. "Very impressive," he said grudgingly.

"Here!" Marty handed Alex a coconut. "Have a drink. It's on the house!"

Alex took a sip.

"Ewwww!" he said, spitting it out again. "This is sea water!"

"You're not supposed to *drink* it," Marty said jovially. "This is only until the plumbing's done. Hey, you all look hungry. How would you like some of nature's goodness?"

Three pairs of eyes lit up.

"You have *food?*" Gloria breathed.

"The fun side special coming up!" Marty told her. "Seaweed on a stick!"

Five minutes later, Alex, Melman, and Gloria were chewing on hunks of green, slimy seaweed stuck on . . . a stick.

"Is it washed?" Melman asked. "I don't think it's washed. . . ."

"Melman," Gloria said. "It's from the ocean. It's been washed its entire life."

"Oh." Melman looked at the seaweed doubtfully.

Marty took a bite. "Could use a little lemon, though," he admitted.

Alex turned to Marty. "You know, I've been thinking," he said slowly. "The people are going to rescue us soon enough, right? In the meantime, maybe we should just give this place a chance. Who knows? We might even enjoy ourselves."

Marty's eyes lit up.

"So," Alex went on. "You got cable in this joint?"

"No cable," Marty said. "But check this out."

Marty pulled a lever and the ceiling opened up. Above them were a zillion twinkling stars, shining against a velvet black background.

"Wow," said Gloria. "Would you look at that."

"That's the thing about the wild," Alex said, sighing. "Everything is overdone."

A shooting star flashed across the sky.

"And defective," Melman said.

Marty shook his head. "It's a shooting star!" he cried. "Quick! Make a wish!"

"I wish I had a thick . . . juicy . . . steak," Alex sighed.

Marty shook his head. "I'm surprised you didn't wish for a rescue boat."

Alex bit his tongue. "Ohhhhh," he said sadly.

Back at lemur headquarters — which happened to be a L10-E airplane with a sign painted on it that said "Madagascar Tours" — Maurice was trying to bring a meeting to order.

Lemurs scampered around the fusilage, chattering excitedly. Maurice stood next to the skeleton of the pilot, trying to get everyone's attention.

"Shhh, everybody," he said, waving his arms. "Calm down! Into your chairs. Yes, everybody, please! You, let go of his tail. Sit down. Somebody separate those two, would you, please? Everybody shhh. Let's get this thing going, okay? All right."

Maurice turned to King Julien, who was sitting in the co-pilot's seat.

"Now presenting Your Royal Highness," Maurice went on, "the illustrious blah blah blah, etc., etc., hurray, let's go."

The lemurs cheered.

King Julien cleared his throat.

The lemurs obediently stopped cheering.

"Now everybody," King Julien began, "we all have great curiosity about our guests, the New York giants."

A lemur raised his hand.

"Yes, Willie?" said King Julien.

"I like them," said Willie.

A few other lemurs nodded excitely.

"I like them, I like them, I liked them first!" Little Mort jumped up and down. "Before I even met them, I liked them. I saw them and I liked them right away."

"Yes, yes," King Julien agreed. "We all like them."

"You hate them compared to how much I like them —" Mort began.

"Oh, shut up, Mort," King Julien said. Mort fell silent. "You are so annoying. . . ." King Julien stopped himself. "Sorry, got to control myself," he muttered. Then he sat up. "No I don't," he said, his head cocked. "I'm the king. I can do whatever I want."

He turned to his lemurs. "Now. For as long as we can remember, we have been attacked and eaten by the dreaded fossa."

"Fossa! fossa! fossa!" screeched the lemurs in a panic.

"The fossa are coming!" one particularly nervous lemur screamed, jumping out one of the plane's windows.

"Please," King Julien held up his hand. "Maurice?"

Maurice stood up. "Shhh! Quiet!" he said commandingly. "C'mon, you all. They are not attacking us this very instant!"

The lemurs settled down again.

"Anyway," King Julien went on, waving for Maurice to sit down, "we all saw the fossa run away from Mr. Alex, right? So my genius plan is this: We will make the New York giants our friends and keep them close. Then, with Mr. Alex protecting us, we'll be safe and never have to worry about the dreaded fossa ever again!"

"I thought of that," King Julien added proudly. "Yes, me. I thought of that."

Lemurs nodded. It was a good plan.

Maurice stood up again. "No, no, no," he said frowning. "Hold on, everybody. I was just thinking. Doesn't anyone wonder why the fossa were so scared of Mr. Alex? I mean, maybe we should be scared, too. Maybe Mr. Alex is even worse than the fossa."

A murmur of concern went through the lemur group.

"I'm telling you, the guy just gives me the heebie-jeebies," Maurice went on.

King Julien sniffed.

"Maurice, you did not raise your hand," he said. "Therefore, your comment will be stricken from the record."

Masikoro the chameleon, who was taking the meeting notes, dutifully erased Maurice's comments.

"Does anyone else have the heebie-jeebies?" King Julien asked sternly, looking around. "No? Good. So shut up. When the New York Giants wake up, we'll make sure they wake up in paradise."

"Laugh, everybody, please," he added.

The lemurs all laughed.

"I am the king. The king says stop," King Julien said next. He loved this game.

The lemurs stopped laughing.

"The king says laugh!"

The lemurs laughed.

"Stop!"

The lemurs stopped . . . all except for Mort, who had been laughing so hard that he had the hiccups.

"I didn't say 'the king says'!" King Julien said gleefully. "You all lose! Now let's get ready for the New York giants!"

CHAPTER EIGHT

It was in the middle of the night in the jungle, and Alex was dreaming about steak.

Everywhere he looked, delicious steak was raining down around him. One of the falling steaks landed on his chest.

Alex grabbed the steak and gave it a hug. Then he licked it.

"Alex?" the steak said.

Alex opened his eyes. He was licking Marty's haunch.

Marty, Gloria, and Melman were staring at him.

"What are you doing?" Marty asked.

"Uh . . . just counting your stripes," Alex said quickly. "Twenty-seven, twenty-eight, twenty-nine, thirty. Hmmmm. Thirty black and only twenty-nine white. Looks like you're black with white stripes after all. Dilemma solved. Good night!"

Alex lay down, rolled over, and pretended to snore.

After a few minutes, Melman, Gloria, and Marty lay down, too.

But something had changed . . . and not one of them could fall asleep.

Above, hidden in a tree, King Julien, Maurice, and about a thousand other lemurs watched Alex and his friends lying together in uneasy silence.

"You see, Maurice?" King Julien whispered. "Mr. Alex was grooming his friend. He is clearly a tender, loving thing. How can you have the heebie-jeebies for Mr. Alex? Look at him. He's so cute and plushy."

Maurice frowned. "I don't think he was grooming, him, Julien," he said. "Looked more like he was tasting him to me."

King Julien pouted. Then he turned his attention down to the animals on the beach.

"Suit yourself," he shrugged. "No matter. Soon we will put my excellent plan into action. All we have to do is wait until they are deep in their sleep."

King Julien sat and waited for about three seconds. "How long is that going to take?" he said impatiently.

Maurice sighed.

The lemurs sat and waited as warm breezes blew wispy clouds across the brilliant, starry sky.

Somewhere in Antarctica, there were no stars to be seen. The wind was howling, the snow was blowing, and a crew of penguins was staring out at their ancestral home in dismay.

"Well, this sucks!" Private said.

Skipper nodded.

There was only one thing to do. . . .

* * *

When Alex woke up the next morning, he had a lemur on his chest.

"Wake up, Mr. Alex!" King Julien was saying. He stared down at Alex. "You suck your thumb?" he asked.

"Aaaagh!" shrieked Alex, jumping to his feet.

Marty, Melman, and Gloria woke up in a hurry. They looked around in shock.

"Where are we?" yelled Alex. "What the heck is going on?"

"Where's the beach?" Melman added in a panic. "Who built a forest?"

"Take it easy!" King Julien said cheerfully. "Don't be alarmed. While you were asleep, we simply took you to our little corner of heaven. "Welcome . . . to paradise!"

The four friends looked around. They weren't in Marty's cabana anymore. They were in the middle of the jungle, at a watering hole. The morning sun shone down. Dozens of trees weighted with colorful, exotic fruit stood in clusters nearby. A gentle breeze rustled the palm leaves.

Yup . . . paradise, all right.

All around them, lemurs were tossing fruit down from the trees, filling baskets and platters to overflowing.

Marty looked around. The vista before him looked just like . . .

"My mural back at the zoo!" Marty took a big bite of mango. "Mmmm. Yummy!"

Alex smiled. "Guess somebody found what they were looking for, huh?"

Marty nodded. Then he stretched.

"Hey! How about once around the park?" he said to Alex. "Let's get our blood pumping. Get these lungs breathing all this fresh air. Who's with me?"

Alex shook his head. "Naw," he began. "I really don't think I —"

His eyes twinkled and he gathered his hind legs beneath him. "GO!" he yelled suddenly.

He shoved Marty aside and took off.

Marty laughed and raced after his friend. "Wanna play rough, huh?"

He dashed in front of Alex, tripping him. "Hey! Got ya there!" Marty laughed.

"Not so fast!" Alex hopped up and tackled Marty.

Then he raced off.

Marty followed. He caught up with Alex and passed him.

Alex was breathing hard. "Okay, Marty!" he gasped. "You win. I'm done!"

Marty turned his Alex as he ran. "C'mon, Alex!" he called. "We were born to run wild. You just have to out that inner lion!"

Alex felt his legs stretch out. Suddenly, he was running faster . . . and faster. He settled into a rhythm. It felt good!

Ahead of him, he could see Marty racing through the clearing. He squinted at the zebra. He stretched his legs and ran even faster.

He caught up with Marty and jumped. "Surprise!" he shouted.

Alex and Marty rolled around and around, finally bumping into a tree. Fruit rained down around them.

"I win!" Alex crowed. "Can't juke the cat! The cat's too quick! Oh, yeah!"

Marty picked himself up and shook his mane. "Yeah, well, normally running isn't a contact sport," he said grouchily.

But Alex ignored him. "Whoo!" he whooped. "I feel good! I feel like a king again!"

Marty grinned. "Now you're talking!"

Alex grabbed a vine that was hanging from the tree. "Yeah!" he shouted. "Let's go wild!"

"Ahhhhhhhhh!"

A Tarzan yell rose up from the jungle as Alex and Marty swung themselves back into the clearing on two sturdy vines. They landed in the middle of the party.

"Whoooo!" Alex gasped. "Man, I feel different! I don't know . . . noogie-noogie-noogie — kind of charged up or something."

Some lemurs scurried up with overflowing platters of fresh fruit.

Gloria was over by the waterfall, holding a coconut cocktail. Lemurs were doing her nails and rubbing her back.

"Marty, Marty, Marty," she crooned. "Like you said, baby — it's crack-a-lackin'!"

Twenty lemurs walked up and down Melman's neck, giving him a shiatsu massage.

"I'm in heaven!" Melman sighed.

Marty smiled. "Whoo, guys! We are taking a walk on the wild side!" He grabbed a fruit and bit into it. "Look at this! It's an all-you-can-eat buffet!"

Strains of dance music played in the background as Alex went over and sniffed at the fruit. "Mmmm," he said. "Something sure smells delicious. . . ."

Marty pricked up his ears at the music. "Lucky I brought my hips," he told Alex. "Let's dance!"

Marty headed towards the music. Alex followed, sniffing the air. *It almost smells like . . . steak*! he thought.

"Marty, there's steak here!" Alex said excitedly "That is steak, baby! Oh, yeah! Steak! I smell steak!"

"You smell steak?" Marty grinned. "Great! I told ya I'd find you some steak!"

A pack of lemurs dragged Marty onto the dance floor.

"Steak? What is this steak?" Alex looked down, and there was King Julien. The lemur looked up at him. "Tell me and I will have my boot lickers whip one up for you."

"Steak?" Alex thought for a minute. "Well . . . it's kinda red on the out side, and moist and firm and just a chewy, chewy . . . that you can get your chunky, chunkies . . . it's all about chunk and the chunk of the chew."

He drooled.

"Yeah, that's right," Marty said, dancing over to Alex. "People make it special for Alex. They love Alex. In fact, back in New York, my man Alex is what you might call a king!"

"King?" King Julien's face fell.

"Yeah," Marty said. "You should see his act!" He turned to Alex. "Come on, Alex. Why don't you show 'em some of your act?"

Alex shook his head. "Oh, no, I don't think I could . . ." He stopped. Why shouldn't he do some of his act? He needed to be sharp for when they were rescued, anyway . . .

"Okay!"

Five minutes later, Marty was blowing into a giant conch shell.

"All right, this is it!" he yelled. He peered around a large palm frond.

"You ready, Alex?" he asked in a big stage whisper.

"Are you ready? Are they ready?" Alex fluffed his mane. He was

feeling good. "'Cause it is showtime, Marty!" He started to warm up his voice. "Arrrgggg. Red leather, yellow leather. Red leather, yellow leather. Red leather, yellow leather . . ."

Alex's eyes were lit with a strange light. His teeth gleamed. Marty suddenly felt a little nervous.

"Well, okay," he said quickly. "Then we better get this show on the road, huh?"

He turned back to the audience of lemurs.

"Ladies and gentlemen, primates of all ages . . . the wild proudly presents the king . . . Alex the lion!"

The lemur band started to play. Alex began to cheer for himself as he always did. But his cheer came out more like a growl.

He coughed and cleared his throat. "Superstar! I'm a Superstar!" he said to himself.

Then he hopped up onto a large rock and struck a pose, his mane blowing in the breeze.

"The king is in the house!" Marty shouted proudly.

Lemurs cheered. A few of them fanned giant palm leaves, making Alex's mane blow. Others blew brightly colored flower petals out of bamboo sticks. The petals floated through the air like fireworks.

"Uh, king?" sniffed King Julien. "Where is his crown? I don't see a crown. I have a crown . . . a big one. Look at it." King Julien peered up. "Do I have it on?"

Alex was doing pushups for the crowd.

"Do the roar, man!" Marty called. "Do the roar!"

Alex opened his mouth. And for the first time in his life, he let out a *huge* lion roar . . . a roar of a lion in the wild.

The lemurs cheered even louder. Alex smiled, a little dazed.

Marty hopped up and down in excitement. "I've never heard *that* one before!" he yelled. "Yeah! Go wild, man! Come on!"

He turned to the lemurs. "Break out the wave!"

A row of lemurs did the wave.

Alex's claws popped out.

He wasn't seeing lemurs. He was seeing a sea of steaks, doing the wave just for him — big, fat, juicy steaks! And the biggest, fattest, juiciest steak of all was —

"YOOOOOOOAAAAAAGH!" Marty shrieked.

Alex blinked.

Marty whirled around and stared at Alex, horrified.

"Excuse me," he said. "You're biting my butt."

"No I'm not!" Alex mumbled, his mouth still full of Marty.

"Yes you are!" Marty shouted, pulling away.

Alex sat up, his eyes wide with shock. "No I didn't! Did I?" he said.

Marty turned to Gloria and Melman. "Did you all see that? He just bit me on the butt!" Then he turned back to Alex. "What the heck is wrong with you? Why'd you bite me?"

Maurice tapped Marty on the flank. "It is because you are his din-ner," he explained.

Alex, Marty, Melman, and Gloria's mouths dropped open. "Excuse me?" Gloria said.

Maurice turned to Julien. "The party's over, Julien," he said soberly. "Your brilliant plan has failed."

Alex blinked. "What are you talking about?"

Maurice pointed to Alex. "Your friend here," he told the others, "is what you'd call a deluxe model hunting and eating machine. Allow me to demonstrate."

Maurice moved behind Alex and pulled his tail. Alex dropped onto all fours as Maurice pointed out his features.

"Low profile quadro-pedal suspension with all-weather treads for hot pursuit of prey," Maurice began, kicking Alex's front paw.

"Ow!" Alex said.

Maurice picked up the paw and punched the pads. Alex's claws sprang out.

"Claws!" Maurice said. "Made of hardened keratin. Can rip open your prey like an overripe mango. Now, let's look under the hood. . . ."

Maurice stuck his fingers into Alex nose. The lion's mouth popped open like the trunk of a car.

"Teeth!" Maurice pointed out. "Front row: incisors for tearing. Back row: molars for grinding."

Maurice reached into Alex's mouth and pulled out a snow globe. "What the heck is this doing in there?"

"Happy birthday, Gloria," Alex said.

Maurice slammed Alex's mouth shut. "But that's not all," he said. "Whiskers! Advanced guidance system."

"Ow!" yelled Alex. "Don't pull!"

"Ears!" Maurice screamed into Alex's ears. "Can detect the sound of a blood-sucking leach at a hundred yards!"

"Aaaah!" Alex jumped a foot. "Too loud! Too loud!"

"Eyes!" Maurice went on. "Adapted for night vision." He poked Alex in the eye.

"Ouch!" Alex protested.

Maurice leapt to the ground and yanked on Alex's tail. "Tail!" he said. "For stabilization!"

"Hey!" Alex said angrily. "Don't pull the tail!"

"These are his tools!" Maurice finished. "Designed exclusively by nature."

"Tools?" Marty scratched his head. "Tools for what?"

"Tools for stalking and hunting and then tearing apart his poor undeserving steak," King Julien explained sadly.

"Which is you," Maurice added.

"Me?!" Marty gasped.

Gloria shook her head. "Oh, get out of here," she said.

"And especially you, too," Maurice said, nodding. "And the Melman."

King Julien nodded. "We are all steak!" he said gloomily. "Everyone who is steak, raise your hands."

Each and every lemur raised his or her hand.

"I'm steak! I'm steak!" Mort said happily. "Me, me, me!"

Alex turned away in horror as the truth started to slowly sink in.

"The Mr. Alex is like the fossa," King Julien went on, "a savage beast who cannot resist his calling to hunt the weak and cute and defenseless. Naughty, naughty!"

"Yeah," Maurice said. "We call it the grossly unfair oval of life."

Alex stared at all of them. They all looked like steaks to him now — each and every one of them. Even Marty . . . his best friend . . . his buddy, his pal . . . was a steak!

Maurice turned to Marty. "Mr. Alex belongs with his own kind, on the fossa side of the island," he said, not unkindly.

"By the power vested in me by the law of the jungle, blah, blah, blah —" King Julien pointed at Alex. "Be gone!" he commanded.

Gloria stepped in front of Alex. "Wait a minute," she said firmly. "We are not just going to stand here and let Alex leave."

"Of course not!" King Julien nodded. "We will hide in the bushes."

Marty stared at Alex. "C'mon," he said pleadingly. "Do I look like a steak to you?"

Alex turned and looked at Marty — the guy he had grown up with, the guy with whom he had spent just about every waking moment of his life.

All he could see was a giant rib eye.

"Yeah," he said hoarsely.

"See?" Marty turned to King Julien. "I told you I don't look like —"

Then he registered what Alex had said. "Wait, wait," he said nervously. "What did you say?"

Alex licked his lips. "Oh, yeah!" he breathed. He dropped down onto all fours, a wild looked in his eyes.

"He's going savage!" Mort screamed.

"Run for your lives!" King Julien screeched.

As the lemurs backed away, Alex lunged toward Marty.

"Marty! Run!" shrieked Gloria.

Gloria, Marty, and Melman turned and ran. Alex took off after them. He honed in on the steak that was Marty. He was closing the gap. He was inches away. He opened his jaws and —

SMACK. A coconut hit him on the head.

Alex collapsed in a heap as Marty and the others ran into the jungle.

Above Alex's body, sitting in a tree, were Julien and Maurice. Julien nodded admiringly.

"A bull's-eye. Excellent shot," he said to Maurice.

Down on the ground, Alex sat up and rubbed his head. Before his eyes, he saw the fleeing steak turn into his best friend — his buddy, his pal — Marty.

"Marty!" Alex groaned. "What is wrong with me? What have I done?"

He dug his claws into his scalp.

"Owww!" He held his paws in front of his face. His claws retracted with a *click*.

"It's true," Alex whispered. "I'm a monster. I've got to get out of here!"

And he stood up and sadly slunk off into the jungle.

CHAPTER NINE

Gloria, Melman, and Marty trudged back to the beach. Everywhere Marty looked, the drama of predator and prey was being played out. A Venus flytrap snapped shut over a helpless fly. A small mouse, racing through the underbrush, was eaten by a snake, which in turn was devoured by a swooping hawk.

It was a place where lions and zebras couldn't be friends.

"This wasn't how the wild was supposed to be," Marty said plaintively. "I was so wrong . . . about everything. My dream of the wild was a fantasy. Because of me, everything is ruined. If only I could turn back the clock. . . ."

Suddenly, a sound like a giant klaxon horn broke into Marty's gloomy thoughts.

BRAAAAAAAP!

"Gloria!" Melman said, shocked. "What did *you* have for lunch?"

"That wasn't me," Gloria said. She pricked up her ears. "That was . . . the boat." She stopped suddenly. "The *boat*!!!!"

"The boat! The boat's come looking for us!" Marty started to run. "C'mon, guys! We gotta flag it down!"

When Marty, Melman, and Gloria erupted, panting, onto the beach, they were just in time to see their ship sailing past the island.

"There it is!" Marty yelled.

"Over here!" they three friends screamed, waving frantically at the ship. "Help! Helllllp!"

Gloria and Marty scrambled on top of Melman.

"Give me a lift, Melman!" Gloria screamed. "Lift me up, lift me up!" She scanned the horizon, looking for the ship. When she saw it, she waved her arms again. "Over here! This way! Stand still, Melman —"

Melman was staggering, trying to keep his footing. As he stumbled around, Gloria and Marty lost their hold on his neck and came crashing down onto the beach.

"AHHHHHHHHH!"

BRAAAAAAAAAP!

Gloria stood up, spitting out sand.

"Look!" She craned her neck to see. "It's turning! It's coming back! It's coming back!"

"Yeah! This way! C'mon! C'mon, baby!" Melman cried.

"We are going home!" Gloria crowed.

"Yes! Yes, yes!" Melman shouted.

Marty turned and looked back into the jungle.

"Wait a minute!" he said. "What about Alex? We can't just leave him here. You guys flag down that boat. I'll go get him."

"Whoa, hold on there!" Gloria stared at Marty, shocked. "You can't go back there. He bit you on your butt, for crying out loud."

"Come on, I know Alex!" Marty insisted. "He hears we're rescued, he'll snap out of it."

Gloria shook her massive head. "This is no time for heroics, Marty. Let's just think this through."

Melman thought hard. "Maybe the people can help us," he finally volunteered.

Gloria nodded excitedly. "Melman's right. The people will know what to do! Now, c'mon, we gotta flag down that boat! Over —" She turned toward shore again. "Here?" she finished, staring in alarm.

The ship was steaming toward the beach at full speed.

BAAAAAAAAAP!!!

Melman, Gloria, and Marty scattered as the ship, hooting its horn like crazy, ploughed up onto the sand and ground to a halt.

An anchor dropped down from the deck and hit the sand with a thud.

The penguins slid down after it.

Skipper looked around at the beautiful, sandy beach, the blue water, the waving palm trees . . .

"Now, *this* is more like it!" he said.

Gloria stared at him, shocked.

"You?" she gasped. "Where are the people?"

Skipper turned to look at Gloria. "Hey!" he said. "I know you two. Where are the psychotic lion and our monochromatic friend?"

Gloria and Melman turned to find Marty.

But he was gone.

"Where *is* Marty?" Melman said.

"He's gone back for Alex!" Gloria groaned. "He's gonna get himself killed!"

"Or worse," Melman moaned.

"What's worse than killed?" Gloria asked.

"You'd be surprised, senorita," Skipper said wisely. "Well, boys. Our monochromatic friend is in danger. Looks like we've got a job to do. . . ."

He turned to Private, who took out a crayon and a pad of paper.

"Captain's log," Skipper dictated. "Embarking into hostile environment. Kowalski! We've got to win the hearts and minds of the natives. Rico! We'll need special tactical equipment. Will face extreme peril. Private probably won't survive. . . ."

Private gulped and snapped off the tip of his crayon.

On the other side of the island, Marty was following Alex's trail through the jungle.

Unseen by him, fossa eyes followed his every move.

"Alex!" he called. "Alex! Come out, Alex! The boat is here! We can go home!"

Lightning flashed, and a rumble of thunder split the silence. Marty looked up worriedly at the sky.

CHAPTER TEN

Two hundred yards away, Alex was dozing fitfully in a cage he had made for himself — complete with wooden spikes, a moat, a small hut, and a big rock. It looked a lot like his home in New York.

Lightning flashed again. In his dream, Alex saw the glare of flashbulbs popping. He blinked. Crowds of people gathered around him. "Alex! Alex! Alex!" they chanted.

Alex stretched and stood up, smiling happily.

Then the crowds vanished.

"Alex? Alex?"

Alex woke up, blinking. It was only Marty, calling his name.

Alex rolled over. "Marty?" he said.

Marty took a deep breath. Then he squeezed through the bars of Alex's makeshift cage and walked up to Alex.

Alex backed away until he was standing against the rock.

Marty swallowed. "Snap out of it, Alex," he said. "Guess what? The boat came back!"

Alex shook his head. "Marty, go away," he said.

"But we can go home!" Marty said. "It's what you've wanted from the moment we got here!"

Alex growled softly. "For once in your life, face reality," he said

quietly. "New York was a lie. It was all just an act. An act that packed them in five times a day, but just an act."

Marty stared. "But Alex . . ." He moved closer.

Alex held up his paw. His claws snapped out with a scary clicking sound.

"See what's happening?" he moaned. "I can't control it. And you feel it, too. I mean, look at your legs."

Marty looked down. His legs were shaking, and his knees were knocking together.

"You want to run, and I want to chase you," Alex went on. "It's only a matter of time before . . ."

He turned and faced the rock.

"Stay away from me, Marty," he whispered. "Everything's changed. I'm a monster."

Alex sniffed. Then he slunk into his makeshift hut.

Marty followed. "Alex," he called after his friend. "You're no monster. I'll tell you what you are. You're the best friend a guy could have."

From inside the hut, there was only silence. But a soft, rustling sound filled the air around Alex's cage.

It was the fossa, closing in.

Marty didn't hear them. He was focused on Alex.

He sat down on a nearby rock.

"Okay, fine," he said loudly. "If you're staying, then I'm staying too. I don't care where we live as long as it's in the same neigborhood."

The hungry fossa had surrounded the patient zebra.

Marty finally noticed them.

"Uh, Alex?" he said, calling back to the rock. "Could you come out here for a minute? Alex?? Hey, Alex? Little help? Alex? AAAAAAAGH!"

Marty leaped over a fossa and ran fast. The fossa snarled and raced after him.

Alex stepped out of his hut and looked around.

Marty was nowhere to be seen.

But in the distance, he heard his friend's voice crying out to him.

"Alex!" Marty was screaming. "HEEEEEEEELP!"

Marty galloped through the jungle, the fossa close behind him. Ahead of him was a clearing. *Gotta find a way out!* he thought desperately as he raced into a large canyon full of limestone formations. He gasped for breath as his hooves pounded on the rocky surface. The fossa loped behind him, easily keeping up.

"Help me!" Marty cried desperately. "Anybody! Help me! Somebody! Help!"

A fossa leaped lightly in front of Marty, blocking his path. The exhausted zebra skidded to a halt and whirled around.

Hungry fossa were everywhere. He was surrounded.

The fossa started to close in.

"You don't want to be eating me now," Marty said quickly. "I've got mad zebra disease. Yeah! I'm mad! Watch out! One bite of me and you'll go crazy —"

The fossa pounced. Marty disappeared beneath their churning bodies —

A bloodcurdling scream stopped the fossa in their tracks.

Marty looked up. Melman swung toward him on a vine, legs flailing. He reached down and picked up Marty from the surprised fossa.

"I've got him! I've got him!" Melman said excitedly.

"What's the plan?" Marty asked.

"Run!" Gloria yelled.

An army of fossa was running toward them.

"Fossa eat! Fossa kill! Fossa eat. Fossa kill!" they chanted.

"Fossa eat. Fossa kill. Fossa eat. Fossa kill." The fossa were almost on them. But just as the fossa were about to pounce, Skipper popped up out of the ground in front of the three zoo friends. He was holding a flare gun.

"Fossa, halt!" Skipper commanded.

The fossa skidded to a halt.

Skipper pointed the flare gun at the sky and fired off a round. The flare zoomed into the sky and exploded in a flash of light.

The fossa stood and stared.

"Fossa ooooh. Fossa aaaaah!" they said admiringly.

From the other side of the jungle, King Julien and Maurice saw the flare.

"Look, Maurice!" King Julien said excitedly. "There's the signal!"

As the fossa watched, the rest of the penguins converged on the scene. They carried the ship's wheel, a number of other parts, and Mort.

Quick as lightning, they set up their trap. The fossa blinked, confused.

Kowalski baited the trap . . . with Mort. He put the little lemur on a plate with whipped cream and a cherry on top of him.

"Come and get it!" Mort said coyly.

The fossa drooled. Then they pounced on Mort. But as they did . . . the penguins started the ship's wheel spinning. Fossa were slammed by the wheel and went flying in all directions.

More fossa appeared. But up above them, a sputtering noise could be heard. And then, the old Madagascar Tours plane flew into view, piloted by Maurice and King Julien.

In the plane, King Julien spoke into the microphone.

"Attention," he announced. "Due to the short duration of this flight, there will be no beverage service."

A bunch of lemurs, sitting in the back of the plane holding coconuts and melons, all groaned.

"Bombs away!" King Julien announced.

Maurice took the plane into a dive, and the lemurs threw a barrage of coconuts and melons out the window. These crashed onto the fossa below and knocked many of them out.

The plane circled around and made ready for another run.

The animals and the penguins continued to battle the fossa. The fight was ferocious. Gloria butted fossa with her head as Melman smashed them with his hooves. Marty whirled and kicked.

But just as the New Yorkers and the penguin crew thought they were getting ahead, more fossa joined the fray.

"There are too many of them!" Gloria gasped, swatting fossa left and right. Three more jumped on her back.

Suddenly, a bone-rattling roar split the air.

Alex bounded into the clearing.

Marty poked his head up and looked at Alex. The lion's face was wild. He snarled.

"Alex?" Marty said.

Alex growled.

Uh-oh, Marty thought.

Alex advanced on the group of fossa. "Alex eat! Alex kill!" he roared. "This one's mine!" He lashed out at one of the fossa, his claws extended. The look in his eye was pure predator.

"Alex eat! Alex kill!" he roared again.

The fossa backed off.

Marty stared at Alex in fascinated horror. Then he shut his eyes. If this was how it was going to end . . .

"Psst, Marty," Alex whispered. "It's showtime."

Marty opened one eye. Alex smiled.

"Thanks for not giving up on me, Marty," Alex said. "You're a real *mensch*."

"You know?" Marty said. "If I knew what *mensch* meant, I bet I'd be touched."

Behind Alex, more and more fossa emerged from the jungle.

"We're getting out of here," Alex whispered. "Just go with me. Like I said . . . it's showtime!"

Alex picked up Marty and threw him over his shoulder. "Mine!" he roared to the fossa. "Mine! My kill! All mine!"

Marty moaned loudly. "Oh. Don't eat me, Mr. Lion! I'm too young to die!"

"Be quiet, you," Alex said ferociously.

Alex looked at Gloria and Melman and winked. They were overjoyed that Alex was putting on an act and quickly began to help.

"Oh no! It's the king of all beasts. He's come to destroy us all!" Gloria wailed.

Alex kept backing away from the fossa. "Fear me . . . ow!" he said, trying to sound regal. "The king of the beasts . . ." Marty landed a particularly painful blow. "Hey, would you take it easy?" he whispered to the

zebra. He turned back to the fossa again. "Savagery beyond comprehension . . ." he went on.

"Let me go! Let me go! Help! Help!" Marty hollered.

"Resistance is futile! My ferocity is unparalleled!" Alex proclaimed.

"Somebody call the cops!" Marty shrieked. "Help me! Lemme go! Lemme go!"

For a moment, the fossa just stood there, dumbfounded. Then they remembered that they were hungry, and snarled menancingly.

Alex had had it.

He let out an enormous ROAR! He drove the fossa back, back, back until they were at the edge of the clearing.

The fossa stood there, cowering in fear.

"Yeah!" Marty cheered.

Alex paced back and forth, glaring at the fossa.

"Resistance is futile," he said. "This is my territory. I never want to see any of you on my side of this island again!"

Alex roared. The fossa slunk off with their tails between their legs.

"You the cat!" Marty cheered.

Then the four friends shared a big, happy hug.

King Julien, Maurice, and the other lemurs in the plane grabbed a parachute and jumped out of the plane. The plane crashed into the jungle as the parachute gently floated to earth.

Other lemurs flowed out of the jungle, crowding around Alex and cheering. "The new king of the jungle!" Marty cried proudly. "Alex the lion!"

Alex bowed modestly. His heart swelled. This was the first time he had ever heard people cheering because of who he was and what he had done. It made him feel great.

Nearby, Skipper stood on top of a pile of unconscious fossa.

"I hereby declare this New Antarctica!" he said. "Rico?"

Rico took out a rubber band and snapped it at one of the fossa's tails. The tail rose, a white surrender flag attached to it. The penguins stood, posing, on the pile of fossa as Private took their pictures.

"Psychotic," Alex said, shaking his head.

A few hours later, everyone was on the beach, sitting around a long banquet table in front of Marty's cabana. Alex sat at the head of the table in a bamboo throne.

"Rico! Ready the tuna," Skipper called.

Alex opened his mouth, and Skipper popped something into it using a long pair of chopsticks.

"Never met a kit that didn't love fishy," Skipper declared.

Alex chewed slowly. Everyone stared at him in anticipation.

"And?" Marty asked.

"Well?" Gloria added.

"Pretty good, right?" Melman said hopefully.

"Tell us! Tell us! This is getting boring!" King Julien commanded.

A smile spread across Alex's face.

"Steak may be fine. But sushi's divine!" Alex said.

Everyone cheered.

"Rico? More yellowtail for the psycho!" Skipper called.

A few yards away on the beach, Rico was at his sushi station. His knife sliced with blinding speed. Soon, a large platter of sushi was ready. He placed it in front of Alex, who smiled happily.

Marty raised a coconut cup.

"A toast!" he said. Everyone raised his or her cups.

"Now, he may be a pain in the butt sometimes," Marty began. "Trust me, I know."

He glanced down at his butt, which had a big bandage on it. Everyone laughed.

"But, this cat," Marty went on, "whose heart is bigger than his stomach, proved to me, without a doubt, what it means to be a good friend." Marty nodded at Alex. "To Alex," he said solemnly.

"To Alex!" the crowd roared.

Everyone took a drink from his or her cup. Then they all spit it out again.

It was still saltwater.

King Julien stood on the table and banged a cup with a spoon.

"Yes, yes," he said. "I have an announcement to make. So shut up! Everyone, please. Thank you. After much deep and profound brain things, I have decided that a king is not a king unless he has a crown. From one king to another, I'm giving Alex my crown. A little something to remember us in Madagascar."

King Julien took his crown and placed it on Alex's head. The lemurs all cheered.

"Mada-who-scar?" Marty asked.

"Mada-what-scar?" Melman echoed.

"Madagascar?" Gloria raised her eyebrows.

"Where do you think you are, you big baby?" King Julien crooned to her. "San Diego?"

Alex blushed.

"No, no, I couldn't," he said, taking off the crown. "This is very nice, but I don't want to take your crown."

"That's okay," King Julien said cheerfully, pulling out an elaborate crown that was about three times larger than his other one. "I have a bigger crown. It's got tassels."

Later, the four friends stood on the ship, waving to the lemurs on the beach. "I don't care where we go as long as we're together," Alex said to Marty.

Meanwhile, the penguins looked over from their beach towels. "Don't you think we should tell them that the boat's out of gas?" Private asked Skipper.

The lemurs all cheered wildly.

THE END

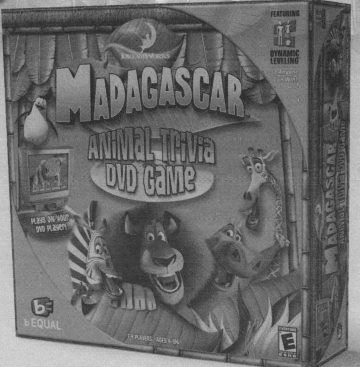